"You want to die? Such a pretty young thing?"

"You won't kill me. Then you'd never know," Maggie rasped.

"I don't wan_____ I have to."

"I..." she sta_____

She felt his _____ caught his attention past the railing down on the beach, his hand still pressing her windpipe. "Who's the cowboy?"

Liam, she thought with a surge of hope. He'd followed her.

She wriggled but he tightened his grip, too, nearly shutting off her oxygen. "You give me what I want and don't involve anyone else, or you know what will happen. It would be so easy."

She was too oxygen deprived to reply.

"Hey," Liam shouted from down below. "Get your hands off her."

Without warning, the man released her and raced away down the stairs. The sudden movement sent her staggering. Her hips impacted the rusted railing. Gulping for air, it took a second for her brain to register that the railing had given way as she fell backward into nothing.

Dana Mentink is a national bestselling author. She has been honored to win two Carol Awards, a HOLT Medallion and an RT Reviewers' Choice Best Book Award. She's authored more than thirty novels to date for Love Inspired Suspense and Harlequin Heartwarming. Dana loves feedback from her readers. Contact her at danamentink.com.

Books by Dana Mentink

Love Inspired Suspense

Roughwater Ranch Cowboys

Danger on the Ranch
Deadly Christmas Pretense

Gold Country Cowboys

Cowboy Christmas Guardian
Treacherous Trails
Cowboy Bodyguard
Lost Christmas Memories

Pacific Coast Private Eyes

Dangerous Tidings
Seaside Secrets
Abducted
Dangerous Testimony

True Blue K-9 Unit

Shield of Protection
Act of Valor

Visit the Author Profile page at Harlequin.com for more titles.

DEADLY CHRISTMAS PRETENSE

DANA MENTINK

HARLEQUIN® LOVE INSPIRED® SUSPENSE

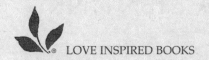 LOVE INSPIRED BOOKS

Recycling programs for this product may not exist in your area.

ISBN-13: 978-1-335-67932-1

Deadly Christmas Pretense

Copyright © 2019 by Dana Mentink

All rights reserved. Except for use in any review, the reproduction or utilization of this work in whole or in part in any form by any electronic, mechanical or other means, now known or hereafter invented, including xerography, photocopying and recording, or in any information storage or retrieval system, is forbidden without the written permission of the editorial office, Love Inspired Books, 195 Broadway, New York, NY 10007 U.S.A.

This is a work of fiction. Names, characters, places and incidents are either the product of the author's imagination or are used fictitiously, and any resemblance to actual persons, living or dead, business establishments, events or locales is entirely coincidental.

This edition published by arrangement with Love Inspired Books.

® and TM are trademarks of Love Inspired Books, used under license. Trademarks indicated with ® are registered in the United States Patent and Trademark Office, the Canadian Intellectual Property Office and in other countries.

www.Harlequin.com

Printed in U.S.A.

In God I will praise his word, in God I have put my trust;
I will not fear what flesh can do unto me.
–*Psalm* 56:4

Dedicated to my parents, Bob and Lisa,
who taught their children what love looks like.

ONE

Maggie Lofton punched the speed in her twin sister's Corvette as a car rounded the corner behind her a little too fast. The twisting road cut along California's central coast was lit only by the moon and her headlights. *Was the person behind her a random stranger or the man she'd been warned about?* Tammy's terrified phone conversation from late the night before rang in Maggie's memory.

"I took something from my boss's house...but I had a good reason. I hid it in Driftwood with someone I trust. You have to get it before his nephew Virgil Salvador does."

"His nephew?" Maggie had tried. *"Why would he...?"*

"Mags, I'm in trouble. Deep trouble."

"The police..."

"No. I'll be arrested. Just pick up my car at Fine Motors Garage and meet me at the lighthouse near the Roughwater Ranch on Thurs-

day night. I'll tell you everything. Don't talk to anyone. No police. Please, Mags."

"Where are you now?"

"I'm safe."

Maggie had gripped the phone tightly at the fear in her sister's voice. Then the call had been abruptly cut off.

Oh, Tammy. Why do you get yourself into these jams?

A smile quirked her face as she imagined Tammy's reply. "Because I fire first then aim, just like Daddy always says."

Everything from bad romances, getting kicked out of her apartment, taking jobs that sounded too good to be true and were—Tammy had fallen into all of them and Maggie had been there to pick up the pieces. As she would be this time as well, if she could just figure out what new kind of trouble Tammy had landed herself in.

The car behind her edged closer, further proof that it wasn't someone out for a leisurely evening drive. Was it Virgil, the nephew? She knew Tammy had taken a job caring for the elderly Bill Salvador in the nearby town of Sand Bar, but Maggie had never met Bill or his nephew.

The whole situation made no sense.

She had to get away from whoever it was long enough to make the meeting with Tammy and sort out the details. If it was the person her sister feared, he must have caught her trail as she'd blown into town. Further, if he believed the woman driving the green Corvette was Tammy, that meant her sister was still safe, in hiding maybe, waiting for Maggie to arrive for their rendezvous. But if Tammy was fine, why had there been no answer to Maggie's follow-up texts and calls?

The car behind her was large. Black. So close now that the headlights blazed in her rearview mirror. The road was slick from a December frost. Dark. Was that a train whistle? Quickly she rolled down the window as the tires struggled to grip the icy road.

"Don't they believe in streetlights here in Driftwood?" she mumbled, pressing harder on the accelerator. She knew every spark plug and bolt in the car, having given it a complete tune-up a month ago after she'd paid the outstanding loan and gotten it out of repossession for her sister.

Per Tammy's instructions, she'd picked it up that very morning from a garage ten miles outside of Sand Dune. There was a formidable dent in the front driver's side and the mechanic said it had been towed in to have the front axle replaced. Clearly, Tammy had been in an accident. Maggie jerked a look in the rearview. Had it been caused by the person currently glued to her bumper? Whoever it was swerved and accelerated. Maggie stomped on the gas. Her pursuer inched closer.

Teeth clenched, she gunned the engine, but it was all she could do to keep the car from lurching off into the split rail fence that now hemmed in both sides of the road. The black vehicle crept over onto the opposite lane until it was level with her driver's door, forcing her within inches of the fence. She could see only a hint of the driver, not enough to decide if it was male or female or to notice any other identifying characteristics.

Whatever they wanted, they weren't going to get it or anything else from Maggie until she knew without question that her sister was safe. *Tam Tam, I got your back, like always.* Tam Tam and Mags, twin sisters and besties for the thirty-two years since they'd arrived together on the planet. That would never change.

The two cars flew almost side by side. The other fender tapped hers and the Vette shuddered and bucked, but she kept it on the road. Panic bit at her. Again came the sound of the train whistle. The speed disoriented her. Was it coming from beyond? Beside? She wanted to slow, but her pursuer had fallen back now, tucking in behind her.

Maggie wasn't a reckless speedster and this all felt like some kind of nightmare. Knuckles white, she held on to the steering wheel and floored it, pulling several car lengths ahead.

Was this man actually trying to kill her?

No, she thought. *He's trying to kill your sister.*

Teeth gritted, Maggie fought the steering wheel and the monstrous fear rising inside her.

Liam Pike dismounted his horse, banged his cowboy hat against his thigh to dislodge the dust and rammed a hand through his thatch of unruly auburn hair. His hip throbbed, courtesy of a 1,200-pound heifer who had taken offense at his notion to move her and the herd to the upper pasture on the Roughwater Ranch.

Now that he was in his midthirties, these little injuries seemed to hang on longer, adding to the collection of pains he'd accumulated in his time as a Green Beret. At least he'd finally managed to wrangle the feisty animal just after sunset, in spite of constant interference from a mutt named Jingles. An early Christmas gift from his sister, Helen, Jingles was rapidly turning out to be a four-legged disaster.

Resting his boot on the lower rail of the fence, Liam surveyed the road that bisected the rich pastureland on one side and the vast Pacific coast on the other. Phone pressed to his good ear, barn jacket shielding him from the California winter, he just barely picked out the distant whistle of the steam train. It eased his mind to know that he could still hear it, at least for the time being. "Little sis, I love you," he said when Helen picked up the phone, "but we gotta talk about this dog." His North Carolina accent was thick, thicker when he was tired and thickest of all when he wanted it to be.

"Isn't he great?" Helen gushed. "The shelter said he'd been there for almost three months and no one wanted him. Can you believe that? They called him Goofy, but Jingles is much better, don't you think, in light of the season?"

"Well, now…"

"He has natural herding instinct, doesn't he? I know he's got Australian shepherd in him."

Liam tried to lasso the conversation back to the point. "Yeah, but that's part of the problem. The critter won't leave me alone. I can't even take a shower without him wanting to join in."

"Excellent. He's devoted to you. You're bonding."

"I don't—"

"Can you call me later, Liam? I need to see to an issue."

An issue…

There was something in her tone…something underlying the jovial teasing that made him think it wasn't a routine situation at the Roughwater Lodge she managed. Prickles danced across the back of his neck. Was something wrong with his baby sister? It was not that long ago, while he was still deployed, that her best friend had been murdered on the Lodge property. Her scars ran deep and raw after the senseless tragedy. His protective instincts buzzed. "What's—?"

"Stop worrying. It's nothing I can't handle, big brother. Go play with your dog." She hung up.

He stared at his phone. Since his father train-wrecked their lives when Liam was a kid, it had been his number one job to care for Helen. Neither his past service as a Green Beret nor his current duties as a cowboy on the sprawling Roughwater Ranch diverted him from tending to her, whether or not she welcomed his assistance.

He heard only a dull hum in his left ear, courtesy of the otosclerosis that had wrecked his hearing and forced him out of military service. He could still get along with a hearing aid in the other, and he prayed every night that God would preserve that sliver of precious auditory function. He jammed the phone into his pocket.

The distant sound of the nine o'clock train whispered again through the December night and he thought with a pang of Tammy, the woman with whom he'd broken up eight months before. He remembered when they'd first started dating, he'd taken her for a ride on that historic steam train and she'd gone pink-cheeked with joy. Dark-haired, boisterous, impulsive Tammy.

Loneliness churned his stomach.

He felt rather than heard the movement behind him. Whirling around, hand on the rifle secured to his saddle, he found Jingles, tongue lolling, one ear up and one down, staring at him with that look of unadulterated adoration that made Liam squirm.

He gaped. "What are you doin' here? I put you out with the respectable herding dogs behind the bunkhouse. Haven't you caused enough trouble for one day?"

Jingles wagged his crooked tail, staring unblinkingly with those inscrutable amber eyes.

Liam folded his arms. "You busted out and followed me, didn'tcha? This has got to stop, dog."

The dog sat, front feet turned outward in that odd pigeon-toed way of his, tail scuffing the grass. "Jingles—" Liam broke off abruptly as he heard the roar of an engine. The vibrations under his feet told him more than his ears. The car was coming too fast along the winding road.

He unlatched the gate and stepped through to get a closer look, Jingles glued to his boot heels.

The car came around the bend, a sleek green bullet. Everything twisted up inside him. He knew that car, a sweet 1972 Chevy Corvette that made his mouth water. Further, he knew the driver, the woman who'd left him and the little town of Driftwood without a backward glance. Tammy Lofton. It could be no one else.

He tracked her progress. Too fast, at the outer edge of control. She was always a bit of a lead foot, but why would she be driving like that? Why here? Now?

Then he saw the second car—dark, also moving rapidly—closing the gap.

"What in the world?" he said aloud, earning an answering yip from the dog he'd temporarily forgotten about. The second fact dropped into his mind, hard and sharp like a collar awl he used for making saddles. The train crossing was two miles ahead. He did the mental math calculations: Tammy's speed, her pursuer, the train. No time to work out much of a plan.

"Stay here," he shouted to Jingles, leaping onto his horse and urging Streak into a gallop toward the crossing. It took a few minutes of hard riding and a sneaky shortcut to catch up with her, Streak flying along the grassy field, above and parallel to her car.

"Tammy!" he hollered. "Stop!"

She was staring out the front window, hair concealing her profile, but the body language read fear, terror even.

"Stop the car," he shouted as loudly as he could manage. "Train!"

But still she drove on, clutching the wheel as the other driver flew around the turn behind her.

Maggie's nerves were screaming as she tried to escape her pursuer, momentarily distracted by a galloping horseman who appeared to be trying to keep pace with her. "One problem at a time," she ground out through gritted teeth. The cowboy would have to wait. The horseman peeled off abruptly and she breathed a smidgen easier.

Glancing at the car behind her, she was thrilled when it dropped back several yards. She let out a shaky breath. *Good*, she thought, breathing slowing a notch. *Go ahead and give up.*

Instead he accelerated and rammed her. The Vette shimmied and slid. She screamed, fingers clawing the wheel for control. He was dropping back again and this time she wasn't about to let him regain the advantage.

The Corvette was practically flying when, without warning, a man leaped onto the road twenty yards ahead. Strangely backlit by the moonlight, she could just make out the silhouette of the horseman who'd been tracking her. He must have taken a detour to cut her off. He was standing on the road, a big guy in a cowboy hat, broad-shouldered, arms held up in warning, like something out of a dream.

"Get out of the way!" she shrieked.

He waved one hand and fired a rifle she hadn't noticed into the air. The shot cracked through the night. She had no choice but to jerk the Corvette around in a wide, bumping arc to avoid running him down. The tires jostled and jumped, taking her off the road. The wheels spun fruitlessly on the frosted grass and she struggled to control the bucking steering wheel. Out of the corner of her eye, she spotted the cowboy, still waving frantically.

What was he doing? Finally the piercing noise and commotion ahead sank into her panicked brain. The clang of signals and flash of lights told her the sickening truth. She was about to drive directly into the path of an oncoming train. She slammed on the brakes but the speed was too much. The whistle pierced the night like a shriek as the Corvette skidded through the signal light, heading straight for the tracks.

She wrenched the wheel and the car whirled in circles, dizzying her. For one heart-stopping moment, she thought her vehicle would hurtle onto the tracks, but it halted some ten feet back, illuminated by the red flashing train lights.

The dark sedan that had been pursuing her came to a sudden stop in a shower of loose rocks, engine idling. She sat, panting, shaking convulsively. In the rearview she saw the cowboy sprint up to her pursuer's car, shouting something. Paralysis stole her ability to move. What should she do? At least one of her car's tires was shredded; she'd heard it explode. Get out and run away from her pursuer and the cowboy? Or stay until the showdown behind her was finished? Should she take her chances with the darkness or the cowboy?

Tammy, what kind of a mess have you gotten us into this time?

She shoved open the door and stepped into a deep rut that sent her to one knee. The cold pierced her body but it hardly registered past the fear. The Corvette had spun and come to a halt facing her pursuer, his headlights blinding her.

"Step away from the car," a voice shouted. It was low and husky. Angry. The cowboy. It had to be. Was he shouting at her? She squatted next to the open driver's-side door. The Vette had skidded to a stop on a grassy clearing. The slight odor of rubber burned her nostrils and she looked down to see the remains of her ruined front tire. She wasn't going to be driving out of there, even if the way wasn't blocked by the sedan. The train barreled on, the noise waning in the distance. For a fleeting moment she wished she could run after it. Instead she was left to cobble together her own escape plan. There was no convenient cover nearby, no structures to hide behind or even trees to conceal her.

The cowboy took a few steps toward the stranger's idling car. "I said get out of the vehicle, mister, unless you want your tires flattened," he shouted again.

While both men were distracted, she should run. But her shaky legs would not cooperate. She clung to the car door, trying to steady her nerves.

A half second later the sedan jerked into Reverse, squealed backward until the driver peeled around and floored it, receding into the distance.

"Coward," she heard the cowboy say.

The sound of his boots plowing through the grass toward her car made her pulse ratchet even higher.

What should she do? What would Tammy do?

He stopped at the other side of her car, silent. More movement sounded in the still night and, all of a sudden, a sturdy white dog raced around the side of the car and barked.

She screamed.

At the sound, the animal lunged forward, swabbed a wet tongue over her forehead and sat, tail wagging.

A hysterical squeal rose to her lips but she kept it in. The boots came closer, until the cowboy rounded the front fender of her car.

"And you teased me about my driving," he said. A strong Southern accent colored his words though she could not make out his features, only the hint of a wide chin and a cowboy hat.

What is he talking about? Teased him?

"Tam?" he said. "You've got some explaining to do."

Tam. The pieces fell into place. This had to be Liam Pike, Tammy's ex-boyfriend.

She leaned her dog-dampened forehead against the metal. What were the chances she'd hit town, nearly get driven off the road, narrowly avoid being hit by a train and finish up by running into her sister's ex?

The dog let loose with a howl.

Maggie felt like doing the same.

TWO

Liam rested the rifle on his shoulder, frustration and confusion warring inside. Wouldn't have been prudent or safe to take a shot and risk return fire with his horse nearby, a nutty dog and Tammy in the vicinity. Still, he would have felt a surge of satisfaction at shooting out the guy's tires. It would've been easy; he was an expert marksman. At least he wasn't losing hold on that.

He reached out a hand and helped her up, her palm freezing cold in his. Tammy Lofton. He'd always admired her impulsivity, the unfettered abandon with which she approached life, but this was sheer recklessness and just plain nuts.

"What in the world are you playing at, Tammy?" Saying her name aloud brought back the anger he'd felt at being unceremoniously dumped for another guy; a computer programmer she'd met when applying for a new job. That stung. "You could have been killed or caused a train wreck."

He realized she'd backed up, palms half raised as if he was an approaching mountain lion. He stopped, blew out a breath and tried for a calmer tone.

"Tammy, it's Liam. Sorry if I scared you. Tell me why that guy is after you. Must be something bad to rile you into forgetting there's a train crossing."

She didn't answer, just stood there frozen.

"Liam," she finally said, almost making it sound like a question. Poor light, scary situation, confusion. Understandable.

"Yeah," he said bitterly. "Glad you remembered my name. Least you can do since we dated for four months. How's the computer programmer?"

"What?" Her voice was softer than he remembered, or maybe he'd begun to lose another level of hearing.

"Did you hit your head?" He felt a glimmer of alarm creeping in. "Tam? You okay?"

"Yes, of course I am. Why did you jump in the road like that?"

"Why...?" He rubbed a palm over his stubbled chin as he struggled for calm. "'Cuz I thought you were gonna crash into the train, that's why," he snapped. "I don't generally welcome people to Driftwood with a rifle in my hand."

But she wasn't even listening. Instead she was inspecting the ruined tire of the Vette. Then she lifted her face to the evening breeze, turning it in the direction of the ocean. She was clearly working out some sort of plan.

"I'm sorry," she said simply.

Was that all she had said or had he missed some? He wasn't feeling like asking her to repeat herself. "Sorry doesn't quite cut it, Tammy. What's going on?" He eased back on his heels and something bumped his leg. He stumbled, winding up on the ground, staring up into the face of Jingles.

Jingles placed a crooked paw on Liam's chest.

"Jingles," Liam yelled. The dog responded by swabbing his face with a warm tongue until Liam finally pushed him off. Jingles sat back, tail skimming the ground in happy lashes. Liam hauled himself to his feet and gathered up the rifle he'd dropped. "Can't ya see I'm in the middle of a situation here?"

Jingles barked.

Liam ignored him this time and ordered a thunderous, "Stay."

He turned back, flabbergasted to find that Tammy had gone, headed off into the night, leaving her disabled Corvette behind.

He looked across the field to where she must have headed: the fog-shrouded beach. "What's gotten into you, Tammy?"

He almost smiled. She should know him well enough to realize she'd piqued both his concern and his curiosity. And Liam Pike had never been one to ignore either.

He whistled once, low and soft, which brought Streak to the fence on quiet hooves. Jingles was on his feet now, too, bottom waggling right along with his tail, apparently convinced his services were needed.

"Just try not to fall off a cliff, okay?"

Jingles barked once and then took up a position behind the horse.

Maggie was grateful there was just enough moonlight glowing through the coastal fog to help her orient herself. She was heading west, toward the beach and the lighthouse. Directly east, near where she'd spun out, must be the vast acreage of the Roughwater Ranch. That explained Liam's arrival. She'd only heard bits and pieces from Tammy, enough to know that their relationship "had no legs," whatever that meant. Imagine running into the guy. He, too, thought she was her sister, thanks to the darkness and the car. At least she knew he wasn't the one Tammy had entrusted her stolen goods with. The poor man sounded as clueless as she felt.

Well, since you've stepped into Tammy's shoes for better or worse, you're going to rub elbows with her acquaintances. She hoped her rendezvous with her sister at the lighthouse would clear the whole thing up. Didn't matter. She'd do whatever she could to pull her sister from the hot water.

But this time things were more serious than unpaid bills or romantic troubles. She thought about the train barreling past, inches from the front of the Corvette.

Way more serious.

Whispering a prayer, she picked up her pace. The grass gave way to a rocky black cliff. Reaching the edge, she peered down onto a rugged beach cloaked in fog. Ahead and to the right she could just make out the steep trail that led down to a jutting promontory of rock where the outline of the lighthouse was visible.

It was a historic structure, no longer in use, though there was a string of Christmas lights twined around the gangway and one small beacon at the top. The lights were courtesy of the ranch owners, Gus and Ginny Knightly, Tammy had told her, to honor the men and women who had served in the navy, as had Gus's father. Maggie had been struck by the story, picturing the couple who believed in honor and respect, two qualities hard to come by these days, it seemed to Maggie.

She picked her way slowly, since the black rock was slippery with condensation and the moonlight partially obscured by fog. The roar of the surf grew louder. They should have met at a café or a gas station, but Tammy always did have a flair for the dramatic. Maggie could never understand it. She could be fully content spending every day bunkered behind a restaurant stove, cooking for patrons like she'd done for years in her parents' café, gleaning plenty of excitement from managing a kitchen. It pained her that she'd had to walk away from several days' wages to come to Driftwood. She'd kissed goodbye money that wouldn't accumulate in her meager bank account, which wouldn't help her with her goal of reopening her parents' restaurant.

You'll get there. The words were stoked with optimism but each year seemed to bring more troubles and financial setbacks. "Eliminate the distractions. Get this thing with Tammy settled and put your nose to the grindstone," she whispered to herself before the wind snatched the words away.

The dial on her father's old watch read nine thirty. Precise down to the second, it was not the loveliest accessory, but Maggie didn't care. It was a part of her father and his legacy, and family was everything.

A rock tumbled loose from somewhere nearby. Maggie froze. Was there someone following? She strained to listen. The wind was howling now, numbing her cheeks. She zipped her thin jacket as far up as it would go, but the chill seeped in anyway.

Finally she made it to the level path that took her to the door of the lighthouse. She listened one more time and checked her phone. Again she dialed Tammy's number, but the call would not go through on this wild, wind-whipped beach. No way to leave a message anyway; her sister had never bothered to set up her voice mail. Her fingers tingled with the cold.

She stared at the device, but the blank screen gave no answers. Had Tammy made it to the lighthouse or not? Perhaps she'd lost her phone. A crack sounded in the night. A rock falling into the ocean? Or something entirely different?

What if her pursuer had waited after the encounter with Liam, retreated, only to find a hiding place from which he could follow her?

She paused with her hand on the wooden door.

What if?

She had no other choice but to go in and follow through on the plan her sister had set in place earlier. Palm clammy, she shoved open the door.

The chilled interior of the old lighthouse smelled of mildew. In the gloom she could barely make out the spiraling metal staircase and cracked plaster walls glazed with moisture. The graffitied interior had been painted over, but more recent messages were scrawled in spray paint.

"Tammy?" she whispered. The only answer was the crash of the surf outside. "Tammy?" she said louder. She let a full two minutes go by before she made a decision. Her sister wasn't there. She could feel it. It was time to get out.

Shoes crunched up the walk outside, heavy, not Tammy's. Prickles of panic erupted up Maggie's spine. There was nowhere to hide, no place to go, except up. Breath held, she scampered quickly up four steps, enough to take her out of the view of the doorway. The creak of the door split the night.

One second. Two…three. Immobile as a statue, she waited.

"Tammy?"

She recoiled deeper into the shadows, her back pressed against the cold plaster. Everything in her shouted at her to run up the staircase, but trapping herself at the top of an abandoned lighthouse would be suicide.

"I know you're here, Tammy. I saw you come in," he said.

She bit her lip.

His tone went soft and friendly with the hint of an East Coast accent. "Listen, I didn't mean to hurt you earlier, back in Sand Bar."

Hurt? Her heart thundered. Was he talking about the car accident?

"I just wanted to talk, but you didn't cooperate. You should have stayed in the hospital, let me help you, not run off into the night."

Hospital? Maggie clamped her teeth together to keep from screaming.

"I was told you'd picked up your Corvette at the garage," he said, "so I guess you weren't too badly hurt. That's good, sweetie."

Sweetie?

Her muscles screamed for escape, but he was between her and the exit. There was only one avenue open: farther up the narrow flight of spiraling metal stairs. She moved as quickly as she could, trying to tread on the stairs where they attached to the wall to minimize squeaking. Maybe he hadn't actually seen her come in. He might be bluffing and give up.

Below her, she heard him move.

Impatience crept into his tone. "I only want

the jewelry. Give it back and forget about it." He paused. "We had a good thing going for a while, Tammy. Don't throw that all away over a misunderstanding." He paused. "I know you're up there… There's no way out. My phone doesn't work here, so I'm guessing yours doesn't, either." He chuckled. "Cat and mouse game."

And I'm the mouse.

Without warning, he charged, metal squealing under his feet, and she had no choice but to sprint up the stairs. Fear powered her, but he was tall and long-legged. He caught her at the top, grabbing her by the wrists and pinning her back against the railing. Her face twisted away from his, eyes blinded by the eerie glare of the lighthouse beacon.

"This is fun, Tammy, the cat and mouse, but I'm short on time."

She writhed in his grip, trying to kick out, wrench her arms free. He was strong and his height gave him leverage.

"Get away from me," she rasped.

He squeezed her wrists until she thought the bones would crack, angling her torso over the railing, the only thing standing between the lantern room behind her and a plummet to the ocean below. Frigid wind tore at her hair, yanking as if it meant to pull her down into the sea. He used his weight to crush her against the metal. Still she could not turn her face to look at him.

"You're going to tell me where you hid the jewelry, who you gave it to. I know it's someone here, someone you know and trust."

Tears of pain gathered in her eyes. "I won't tell you anything."

He pressed harder, his jaw clenched with the effort.

"You want to die? Such a pretty young thing? Splattered all over the rocks?"

"You won't kill me. Then you'd never know," she snapped.

"I don't want to kill you," he said. "But I will if I have to."

"I—" she started.

She felt his body twitch, as if something past the railing had caught his attention down on the beach. "Who's the cowboy?"

Liam, she thought with a surge of hope. He'd followed her.

She wriggled, but he increased the pressure, nearly expelling all the air from her body. "You give me what I want and don't involve anyone else, or you know what will happen. It would be so easy."

She was too oxygen-deprived to reply.

"Hey," Liam shouted from below. "Get your hands off her."

Without warning, the man released her and raced away down the stairs. The sudden movement sent her staggering. Her hips hit the rusted railing. Gulping for air, it took a second for her to register that the railing had given way and she was falling backward. Flailing, her fingers desperately sought for something, anything, to save her life.

THREE

Liam sprinted around to the walkway a few seconds too late to properly neutralize the guy. He got off only a quick rifle shot that skimmed over the goon's shoulder, just enough to scare him. It worked. The guy stumbled in his fear and fell. On the ground, he rolled then dived behind some rocks. When he popped a head up, only the whites of his eyes and teeth shone in the thick darkness.

"Gonna stay and shoot me? She's not gonna hang on for long. Tough choice, right, cowboy?" he called.

Liam gripped the gun, glancing quickly upward to see the shadowy movement on the lighthouse platform. He did not dare look too carefully. "Won't take me long to stop you."

"But you're not that kind of guy, are you? Shooting an unarmed man?"

"Guess you don't know what kind of man I am, do ya?"

"Oh yes, I do." He came up with a handful of sand and hurled it in Liam's direction. Liam flinched and the man took off, running full-on into the night.

Liam had learned when he was seven years old that there was right and there was wrong. The lines blurred at times, particularly in his tenure as a Green Beret, but they were still there, which was why the lunatic was not already dead at Liam's feet. As he ran into the lighthouse and charged the steps two at a time, he wished he hadn't learned that lesson quite so well.

I'll have another showdown with that clown, he told himself.

He heard her gasping, struggling to hold on, as he exploded onto the top level to see her fingers clawed around the broken piece of railing. Flopping onto his stomach, he grabbed her forearms. The angle was bad; the leverage was worse. He couldn't see past the end of his nose, but he hung on for all he was worth.

She wriggled, fingers white and trembling with the effort.

"Can you brace your feet on the wall?" he grunted.

Breathing hard, she shimmied, almost detaching herself from him. He slid one palm down her arm and gathered a bunch of her jacket. "All right. Plan B. You're going to have to let go so I can haul you up."

She whimpered once and the sound went right through him.

"It's okay," he said, trying to gentle his tone. "I promise I'm not going to let you fall."

Fear pinched her mouth, bangs scattered over her eyes. "I can't," she breathed.

The muscles in his shoulders began to blare a steady warning. Though she was petite, barely tall enough to climb up in his truck all the months they were dating, her body was dead-weight and he could not maintain his hold for much longer. He shifted.

"Tam, I know I'm not the guy you wanted to run into just now, but at the moment I'm the only one around. We didn't make it as a couple, but you could always trust me. Isn't that right?"

She stopped struggling and he felt her start to lose her grip.

"Trust me now, Tam. Come on. On three, you're gonna let go. One…"

Her eyes rounded in fear, molten and terrified in the moonlight.

"Two…"

Again the softest whimper, fear again, but edged with resolve this time. She went dead still.

"Three."

She let go. The downward pull strained every muscle in his body, required every iota of strength he possessed not to drop her. Groaning with the effort, he began to command his body backward, pulling one excruciating inch at a time, the platform creaking in protest. Their combined weight added to the ledge already weakened by time and the salt air. How much longer would it hold? Sweat blinded him and he thought his shoulders would dislocate when at last he pulled back just far enough that her torso cleared the busted railing.

She crawled up next to him and collapsed. He rolled onto his back, sweat mingling with the cold winter air, sucking in painful gusts as he recovered. She breathed hard next to him, one shuddering gasp at a time.

Finally she managed to sit up.

"Thank you," she whispered.

"Anytime," he groaned, unable yet to attain a sitting position.

Several more minutes passed before he rustled up the strength to roll over and get painfully to his feet while she did the same.

He let the silence linger for a few more minutes while she stayed there, staring out at the ocean without seeing it, the beacon painting them in odd yellow light.

"Tam, why is that guy trying to kill you?" he said finally.

She jerked when he said her name. "I don't know."

He raised an eyebrow. "I think you probably have a general idea."

"No."

He rolled a tentative shoulder to make sure it was still in the socket. "All right. Well, let's take a ride over to Danny Patron at the Driftwood Police Department, and you can tell him all the things you don't know."

"I have to go."

He blinked. "When someone tries to run you down and knock you off a lighthouse, the correct countermeasure is to solicit the help of law enforcement personnel. They live for this kind of stuff."

"Thank you. For what you did, I mean. I—I mean... I would have..."

"Fallen to your death were it not for the heroic actions of your ex-boyfriend," he finished.

She startled then and a tiny smile shone on her face. Odd, it struck him. Tammy was a blurt-it-out, take-no-prisoners, impulsive woman. But maybe the trauma had subdued her mouth for the moment. "Thank you, Liam."

"You're welcome, now—"

She left him there, mouth open wide like a

dummy's, talking to no one as she jogged down the staircase.

"Hey," he said, hurrying after her as best he could considering he'd probably pulled every muscle in his upper body. "You can't just run off into the night."

Apparently she had not pulled quite as many muscles as he had, since she made it out the front door by the time he caught up.

To his utter lack of surprise, Jingles was waiting. He barked once at Tammy and leaped for Liam, tail wagging.

"All right, all right," he said. "Stand down, would ya?"

She'd used his distraction to make it nearly to the cliff trail before he caught up and stopped her with a hand on her wrist. She jerked around. He heard rather than saw her sharp intake of breath and regretted scaring her. Tammy had never been afraid of anything, to his knowledge, and he hated seeing it in her now. Her wrist was smaller than he remembered, more delicate. He let her go. "Sorry," he said. "Let me take you to the police station. Please."

She stopped at the word *please*. Aunt Ginny would be proud of him for remembering his manners, especially when dealing with a woman who was acting in a completely irrational manner.

She checked her phone, frowning at what she

did or did not see there, and turned away, folding her arms around herself, taking in the long, lonely cliff trail, perhaps.

"Can you…would you give me a ride?" she said softly.

He leaned closer. "How's that?"

"A ride," she said louder.

"Sure, the police—"

"To my trailer?"

"Your trailer? I thought you moved away permanently."

"Kept up the rental."

He wanted to ask if she was planning to stay. He didn't know exactly how he would feel about running into Tammy Lofton again in the small town of Driftwood, but he didn't think the feelings would be good.

"The police—"

"My trailer," she said, more firmly this time. "Can you take me? Otherwise, I'll walk back to the Corvette and change the tire and drive myself."

"Since when would you voluntarily get dirty, Tam?" *And when had she learned to change a tire, for that matter?*

She waited him out and he detested the fact that he already knew he was going to cave. Not like he would leave a woman, any woman, even the last woman on earth he wanted to see, alone in the dark, fixing her own tire, no less.

"Well, all right," he said, "but I'm on record as saying this makes about as much sense as puttin'…"

"A screen door on a submarine?" she finished.

He goggled. "Was gonna say putting socks on a rooster, but same principle. Since when do you spool out the country witticisms? Thought that drove you crazy."

She shrugged. "Never mind. I just want a ride, that's all."

"Fine," he snapped, turning away and whistling for Streak. "But just so you know, you're gonna be riding behind me, followed by a lunatic dog who doesn't know a horse from a hula hoop."

He thought he caught another smile as he climbed painfully into the saddle and lowered an arm down to help her up behind him. When he eased Streak into a trot, she circled her arms around his waist. Gently, he noticed with some appreciation. She seemed comfortable in the saddle. Puzzling, since Tammy stayed as far away from the ranch and horses as she possibly could.

He wanted to fire a couple of questions over his shoulder, but his sides were aching and he figured she was just as uncomfortable. He'd give her a ride to her trailer, but it wasn't going to be the end of things. Not until he had all his questions answered, like who was trying to kill his ex-girlfriend and why?

Maggie clung to Liam's narrow waist as best she could through the pain that pulsed through her ribs. He smelled of leather and hay, a heady combination. She didn't even want to think about how much discomfort he was in after he'd put his own life in danger to save hers. The rocking motion of the horse aggravated her pain and she rested her head against his wide shoulders, trying to control her stampeding thoughts.

She'd almost been killed.

What's more, the stranger—who had to be Virgil—had apparently been responsible for her sister's accident, and now Tammy was on the run. Where? At least the why part was becoming clearer. Tammy had taken jewelry and he was bent on retrieving it. Maggie had no idea why Tammy would have done such a thing, but there had to be a good reason. There had been no messages from her sister when she'd checked. She desperately wanted to look again but she couldn't do that without risking dropping her cell as the horse traveled along.

What exactly was she going to do next? Liam

was right that she should talk to the police, but her sister had specifically asked her not to.

I don't want to kill you...but I will if I have to.

Maggie had heard only a little about Tammy's new job. Guilt licked at her insides. She'd been so busy working insane hours subbing for a cook at a steak house in Arizona, banking every last, sweat-covered dime, that she hadn't really taken the time to reach out to Tammy as often as she should have. Maybe if she had, her impulsive sister would not have detonated her life again.

Next steps, next steps, she chanted to herself as they trotted in view of her sister's trailer parked at the end of the row. Tammy had kept up the rent until she decided to put down more permanent roots; her job as caregiver for Bill Salvador came with a room.

Streak slowed to a walk. A scant few moments remained until she would have to dismount and face a very determined cowboy who she'd gleaned from Tammy was highly intelligent.

What choice did she have but to stall until she knew where her sister was?

Liam reined in the horse and eased off him, not quite disguising the groan as his boots hit the ground. He offered her a calloused palm that all but dwarfed her hand in its strong grasp. She slid out of the saddle, patted the prancing dog and headed up the porch steps. The tiny single-bulb lamp was on, moths circling around.

"Thank you very much," she said as she passed him. "I don't know how else to repay you. Ride safe home."

He'd moved faster than she thought, edging in front of her and leaning a shoulder against the door. "Seems like you haven't answered the pertinent questions."

She stopped. He curved a finger through the belt loop of his jeans and crossed his booted ankles.

"There's nothing else."

He craned forward a bit. "What's that?"

She remembered Tammy had told her something about Liam having hearing loss. "I've told you all I can," she said, louder.

He smiled and thumbed his hat back, the light accentuating his strong jaw. "Aw, now, I don't think that's the full honest truth. We're not exactly strangers. You should talk to me."

The urge rippled through her to tell him, to trust him. But how could she when Tammy had not? When she had no idea whom to trust or where to turn?

She straightened, tipping her chin up to look him in the face since he was a good six inches taller. "I'm not going to tell you anything further."

He blew out a breath. "So you're just gonna stay out here in this trailer, all by your lonesome, when you've almost been hit by a train and dropped off a lighthouse?"

"I'm safe. There are neighbors. I have an alarm." At least, her sister used to have an alarm on her trailer. "I have a cell phone."

"To call the police, whom you don't wanna talk to?"

She waved him off. "I'm tired and I need a shower. I'll be fine."

"All right, then I'm gonna stay here and keep watch. I'll go home and get my truck. Me and Jingles here will bunk in the back seat."

She gritted her teeth. "Not necessary. You're going to leave."

His lips curled in a sassy, slow smile that flicked her pulse higher. "How're you fixing to move two-hundred-plus pounds of good ol' cowboy off your property, Tam?"

She took a step closer. "I'm going to ask you politely, Liam, and you're going to respect my wishes and leave." Silence lengthened between them. Was he that kind of man? The next few seconds would tell.

He huffed out a frustrated breath and she knew she'd won the battle. "All right, then. You read that right. I'd never disrespect a woman, not in this lifetime. I got a lot of sins under my belt, but not that one."

With a sigh, she reached for the door but froze when he put one finger gently on her forearm. The connection held her in place. "You know," he said, his voice a low, rumbling drawl, "there's something different about you, Tam."

She didn't answer. He let his finger remain there for a moment, a spot of warmth in the icy December night. Then he withdrew and walked back to his horse.

The relieved exhale hadn't quite left her lungs when he threw a remark over his shoulder.

"Something's not right here, and I'm gonna worry this bone till I figure it out." He put a finger to his hat in perfect cowboy form and smiled. "Sleep well."

She watched him go with a sinking feeling that Liam Pike would match her determination stride for stride. She may have won the battle but the war was far from over.

Saddle up, Maggie. Rough trail ahead.

FOUR

Liam's almost brother, retired US marshal Mitch Whitehorse, was not prone to smiling. Liam guessed he wouldn't be, either, with a serial killer for a sibling. But since Mitch had put Wade back in prison almost a year prior, married Jane and adopted her son Charlie, his demeanor was downright sanguine. He was loping through the living room of the Roughwater Ranch main house with Charlie on his shoulders, the day after the incident with Tammy, doing loop de loops around the giant Christmas tree.

"Playing horsie?" Liam teased. He gave Charlie a high five, reveling in the joy shining in the little boy's face. He could barely remember life at the ranch before Charlie had arrived, and he didn't much want to.

Mitch cocked his head, the scar on his cheek catching the winter sunlight streaming through the window. "Nah, I'm a train, of course. Anyone can see that. Charlie's excited about riding the Train of Lights next Wednesday."

"Choo choo, Uncle Liam," crooned the three-year-old. The name came out sounding like "Weeum," which made Liam grin every single time.

"Ah. Train. How could I have missed that?"

"You missed a cow, too," Mitch added. "Got her from the lower pasture and returned her to the herd."

Liam jerked. He wanted to blame it on his disastrous new excuse for a herd dog, but it was purely his own preoccupation. He'd spent the early morning, after the feeding duties were done, searching for Tammy Lofton and going so far as to ride to her trailer to check on her. But there'd been no sign of the woman.

"Something you want to get off your chest?"

Liam realized Mitch was watching him closely. It would be the smartest thing to do to unburden himself to Mitch, get his take on the whole situation with Tammy and the guy chasing her. But she'd asked him not to and he'd respect that—for now. "Nah. I was just being careless. Won't happen again."

"Careless is one thing you aren't, brother."

No, he wasn't. It was why he'd earned the nickname Hound Dog from his fellow Green Berets. When he got the whiff of a mission that interested or perplexed him, he'd go after it with methodical zeal and relentless drive.

Aunt Ginny joined them and Mitch hunched down for her to plant a kiss on Charlie's cheek. She did so and handed him a gingerbread cookie. "Your mama called and said you need your bath."

When Charlie frowned, Liam gently poked his arm. "Hey, little cowboy. Christmas parade's tomorrow. Gotta look your best."

The child brightened and Mitch nodded. "Orders from the conductor. Let's chug out of here."

"Choo choo," Charlie said gleefully, clutching his cookie as they galloped to the door, heading for the small house on the ranch hilltop that Aunt Ginny and Uncle Gus had gifted Jane and Mitch for a wedding present.

Ginny had a file of papers tucked under one arm and a laptop under the other. As accountant and joint owner of Roughwater Ranch, she was never far from her paperwork.

"No cookie for me?" Liam said, pulling a mournful pout.

She laughed. "There's a dozen in the kitchen for you. I didn't even bother to wrap them up."

"Too busy?"

"Insanely. Driftwood is swimming in holiday visitors and they all seem to want to stay at the Lodge and tour the ranch while they're here."

"Who wouldn't? Good for business."

Ginny blew out a breath. "Yes. Thank goodness your sister is a brilliant lodge manager."

"That she is. Seen her lately? She didn't return my call this morning."

"Just busy, I'm sure. Speaking of which, Nan called about her saddle. I told her you'd drop it off at the Chuckwagon today."

"Yes, ma'am. I'll do that now."

"And would you take your nutty dog along? He's been staring through the back door whining because he can't find you."

Liam gaped. "I fenced him behind the workshop. How does he keep getting out?"

She heaved a dramatic sigh. "The power of unrequited love."

"Aw, man," he mumbled, striding through the cozy ranch kitchen.

"Help yourself to…" The rest of her phrase died away. He could hear the merriment in her voice. He edged past yet another Christmas tree nestled near the bank of windows that framed the view of the sprawling property and the ocean beyond. The tree lights were twinkling, regardless of the daytime hour. Aunt Ginny insisted they be lit 24/7. She was as eager for Christmas as Charlie was, and Liam loved that about her.

He'd come to the ranch almost three years

prior, at Helen's suggestion, after his discharge from the Berets. He'd applied for a position as a ranch hand and Aunt Ginny and Gus had given him the job and folded him immediately into the family, as they'd done for his sister. They'd been more his parents than anyone else and he still pinched himself that God had blessed him so richly.

Grabbing two cookies from the tray, he flung the door open to see Jingles overcome with joy, dancing on his hind legs. "Down, you mutt," Liam thundered. The dog sat, but all of his parts seemed to vibrate with contained ecstasy. Liam sighed and flung him a gingerbread arm, which Jingles intercepted midair and swallowed, swiping a floppy tongue across his mouth.

"At least you have good taste in cooking." Liam retrieved the repaired saddle from the workshop and loaded it in the back of the truck. When he opened the driver's door, Jingles leaped in and scooted to the passenger seat.

Liam fired up the engine and turned on the radio to a news station. He didn't much care about the chatter but the voices comforted him. The inevitable mental quiz scrolled through his mind. Was the sound fainter? Less distinct? A familiar twist in his stomach started up again. *You can still hear it. You're all right.* But how much longer until he couldn't? The stapedectomy on his left ear had failed to correct the oto-sclerosis that had forced him to leave the Green Berets. He didn't blame God for the misfortune; he'd learned as a kid that life was sometimes a rough ride through bad country. The trick was to gather up all the joy along the way and wait it out until the end. Home with God. A perfect home. The kind he'd always envisioned.

Before he coud drive away, he spotted Chad Jaggert hauling a blue spruce out of the truck and hopped out to help. "Hey," he called, not expecting much of a reply. Younger, leaner, and way quieter than Liam and Mitch, Chad made about as much noise as a mouse wearing slippers. Unless the topic was horses or possibly boats, it was going to be a one-sided conversation. Silent, thoughtful and fiercely loyal, that was Chad, the man Liam considered to be his younger brother.

"Hey," Chad replied, pulling on a pair of leather gloves and shouldering the tree.

"Hasn't Aunt Ginny got enough Christmas trees?"

Chad shrugged. "She wanted it. I got it."

And that about summed up what any of the four— Mitch, Liam, Helen and Chad—would do for Aunt Ginny.

Uncle Gus strode up, accepting his licking

from Jingles. "Another tree?" He grinned. "I'm surprised she's limited herself to five."

"Six," Chad said. "Got one for the tower room yesterday."

Gus laughed outright, pulling off his cowboy hat and scrubbing a hand through his silvered hair. "That woman delights me."

That woman.

Liam thought for a moment of Tammy Lofton. She'd been zany and impulsive, with a fun-loving outlook, but for some reason they just hadn't clicked. He'd had other relationships that didn't work out of course, but when she'd gone, it had left him off balance and uncertain, like a hobbled horse. If he analyzed it, the situation might have affected him especially deeply because the relationship had failed as his hearing loss had accelerated. Good thing he wasn't prone to self-analysis.

Uncle Gus punched him playfully on the shoulder and he realized he'd not heard the last comment. He thumbed his cowboy hat back and offered a grin, which he figured fit the previous tone of the conversation, a trick that often helped him through.

"Listen, if you see your sister, tell her I've got the tables she needed for the festival on Wednesday. I stopped in earlier to see her but she wasn't available."

That made Liam take note. Not returning calls, not available at the Lodge. "Okay," he said. "I'm droppin' off this saddle at the Chuckwagon and then I'm headed over there. Feed's been delivered."

The Roughwater Ranch cattle were grass fed, but years of drought had made it necessary to supplement with hay and alfalfa. Now that they'd gotten some winter rains, the grass was reviving, and the wells and natural springs were also gradually replenishing.

Uncle Gus headed to the kitchen door to open it for Chad. Liam and Jingles headed to the Chuckwagon.

The parking lot was full at half past ten, a sure sign that holiday crowds were building. The two enormous wagon wheels that flanked either side of the wooden doors were twined with tinsel and Christmas music wafted out as he left Jingles in the truck with the window open a few inches.

"Be right back and don't chew the upholstery."

Jingles looked hurt, as though offended he wasn't invited to come along. Liam shouldered the saddle and went inside.

Nan greeted him over the noisy bustle of diners. "Here for breakfast, Liam?"

"No, ma'am. Just delivering your saddle."

"Super, since there's not an empty table in the place. I don't know what I would have done if Tammy hadn't showed up."

"Tammy?"

"Yeah. She came in this morning and I hired her back immediately. She's been an absolute lifesaver." Nan shook her head. "Weird. When she was here last, she was a server only, said she couldn't even boil water, and now it's like she's perfectly at home behind the stove. Even baked the pumpkin pies this morning, before her waitressing shift. I don't know how she doctored the filling, but, man, are they luscious. Why didn't I know she was a kitchen savant?"

Why indeed? He scanned the diners and servers. "Where is she?"

"I'm sending her over to the Lodge with the order of pies for their lunch service. Think she's loading up the van right now."

He thanked her and left the saddle, hurrying back outside. The Chuckwagon van was parked in the back, the rear doors open. Tammy was sliding in the last pastry box, her dark hair draped forward over her eyes. Jeans and a Chuckwagon T-shirt made her look much younger than her thirty-two years—or maybe it was her slender frame and lace-up sneakers.

"Morning," he said.

She jumped, whirling to face him. "Oh…hi."

"Understand you're working here again."

"Um, yes." She slammed the back doors and made to edge by him to the driver's seat. The closer he came, the more the sensation that something was amiss trickled through his gut. "Taking these pies over to the Lodge."

"Right. Can we talk a minute?"

"No, not right now. Delivering, as I said."

She reached for the door and he caught her hand in his. Small fingers, strong and pleasantly toughened from hard work, but tiny and delicate. Strange. He remembered her hands being soft as silk.

"Aw," he said. "You have a half second for one quick question right? For old time's sake?"

She froze, head angled down so the hair shadowed her face. He let go of her hand and slid a finger under her chin, gently tipping it upward. The eyes that greeted his were familiar, the combined green and brown of summer turning to fall. Familiar, but not completely. A halo of gold edged the irises, molten and vibrant. "Tam, your eyes have kind of a green tint, you know," he said slowly. "But now I'm looking close, I see a wash of gold there, like the sun setting into the ocean."

Her throat convulsed as she swallowed. "Uh…" she managed to finally say. "I have to hurry and get back for the lunch rush."

He let the smile ease over his face as he leaned a fraction closer until the brim of his cowboy hat shadowed them both. "Just one question," he murmured.

She tried to look away but again he guided her gaze back to his with the lightest pressure under her chin. The gold was sparked with concern as she stared at him, one lip caught between her teeth.

"Who are you really?" he said.

Caught. Nan and the few patrons who'd assumed she was her sister had asked no questions. Even the man who'd seemed intent on killing her had mistaken her for Tammy. But there was no deceiving the cowboy who stood before her, every inch a stubbled and stubborn man, steely eyed and determined.

She eased back a step, away from the touch of his long, calloused fingers, and folded her arms across her chest, desperately trying to identify an escape route. When she risked a look, he was regarding her from under the brim of his cowboy hat with a half smile that spoke of amusement rather than anger.

"You're not Tammy. What's your name?" he asked.

"Maggie," she mumbled to her shoes.

"A little louder, if you don't mind," he said, cocking his head slightly.

Sucking in a breath, she leveled a square look at him, noting that *his* irises were the color of stonewashed denim.

"My name is Maggie Lofton. I'm Tammy's twin sister."

"You don't say?" Now his smile was wider, as if the information amused him. "Not identical, now that I'm really looking."

His frank stare did not make her uncomfortable for some reason, just worried that she had already messed up on her impromptu investigation.

"Fraternal," she said. "I'm the younger one by two minutes."

He laughed at that and she found herself smiling.

"Tammy told me she had a sister. I don't recall hearing you were twins."

It was Maggie's turn to fix him with a look. "You two dated for four months, didn't you?"

"Yes, ma'am."

"Did you tell her everything about your life?"

That made him blink and look away for a moment, gaze shifting from her to the winter sky. "No," he said. "I guess I didn't."

"Okay, well I'm glad we talked and I'm sorry I wasn't forthcoming right away. I, uh, have a good reason, if that means anything. Um, see you later."

"Uh-uh. You owe me an explanation." The soft drawl in his voice did not lessen the intensity of his command.

She wanted to tell him she owed him nothing, but she recalled the feel of his muscles struggling to haul her up over the lighthouse railing. In fact, she owed him her life. The reality of that made her want to sprint away into the tall green grass that edged the parking area.

"I…" she started to say when his phone rang, too loud. She figured he had it turned up so that he could hear it.

"Hang on one minute, ma'am," he said.

She sighed. "First off, now that you know my real name, you can knock off the ma'am thing. Second, I'm not waiting. I have to go."

But he was already answering the phone. The genial inquisitiveness in his expression turned to concern. "I'm on my way," he told the caller.

She took it as her reprieve until he shoved the phone into the rear pocket of his faded jeans.

"That was my sister, Helen. She asked me to come ASAP to discuss a situation."

"Sounds serious. You should go."

He was silent for a moment, drawing out his keys. He whirled the key ring around his finger, expression calculating in a way that made her squirm. She'd just decided to forget the debt she owed Liam, get into the van and put as much distance as she could between the two of them when he spoke again.

"Helen said she called over here to the Chuckwagon just now and heard I was chatting with you, so she told me to bring you along. That will suit, since you're headed there anyway, right—" he added after a pause "—Maggie?"

FIVE

There seemed to be no choice at all, so Maggie, in the van, followed Liam to the Lodge, wondering the entire ten-mile journey why Liam's sister had summoned her. Tammy had mentioned Helen a few times—they were friends—but Maggie could not imagine what Helen wanted.

At least it had bought her some time to avoid Liam's questions. He'd busted her right and proper. So far she had discovered nothing about whom her sister might have entrusted with the jewelry Virgil Salvador sought so desperately or where her sister might possibly be staying. How much longer would it be before she heard from her?

Tammy, where are you? Tension knotted her already taut muscles even tighter. And something else zinged along her nerves: a strange buzz that had started up when she'd looked into Liam's face as he'd described her eyes... *A wash of gold there, like the sun setting into the ocean.*

Tammy had always been the one to whom men paid attention...her outgoing, bubbly spirit, the long, fashionable hair and trendy outfits. It was just the way things were and it had never caused Maggie a moment of angst. She wasn't the belle of the ball, more like the star of the stove, which suited her just fine. Liam's scrutiny unsettled her. That was all. Who wouldn't be rattled with the current situation?

There was no more time to mull it over as she pulled the van up at her destination. She marveled at the rich wood exterior and peaked roof of the rustic building. Enormous Christmas trees, glittering with ornaments, flanked either side of the substantial front doors. The porch itself housed cozy cushioned benches and pots of crimson poinsettias. Liam caught up to her, Jingles's nails scrabbling on the flagstones in hot pursuit.

He stepped ahead and pulled open the heavy oak door for her. Though his smile was pleasant, concern pinched the corners of his mouth.

"Jingles, you stay out—" Liam didn't finish his sentence before the dog trotted right into the pine-scented lobby.

Giggling, Maggie sailed in, too, leaving Liam grumbling along behind her. The lobby was as glorious as the exterior, all dark woods and comfy seating areas, illuminated by a massive chandelier formed from a collection of antlers. Cheerful clusters of people sipped cider and hot chocolate. The stone fireplace dwarfed the space, the mantel artistically decorated with greenery, crystal icicles and a white porcelain Nativity scene. Yet another Christmas tree, this one decorated with gold and silver balls, stood sentry near the front desk.

A woman with auburn hair twisted into a neat chignon, despite the pencil skewered through the elegant twist, hurried out to meet them. She blinked when she saw Maggie before she extended a manicured hand. "I'm Helen, Liam's sister."

Liam didn't waste time on the niceties. "What's wrong? Why did you need to see us both? How did you know she was Maggie, not Tammy?"

"Stand down, soldier," she said. "Come with me." She led them behind the front desk, nodding pleasantly to the couple checking in with the young employee. "Welcome to Roughwater Lodge," she called out before they entered a quiet hallway and climbed a narrow flight of stairs.

On the way, Maggie caught the scent of something savory cooking in the kitchen. Her brain automatically sorted the scents into their elements: chicken, garlic, thyme, perhaps bay leaves and white onion.

"We're completely booked," Helen was saying. "My room was the only place."

"Place for what?" Liam said, scooping up Jingles as he tried to scamper ahead of them. "This dog has zero manners."

"Devoted, just like I said," Helen quipped over her shoulder. She opened a door at the top of the stairs that led to a charming sitting room impeccably decorated in elegant creams with touches of green and exposed wood beams overhead. A real Christmas tree scented the room, ornamented with white lights and what looked to be tiny, handcrafted leather ornaments, each a different animal.

"Stay here for a second. I'll be right back."

"Helen…" Liam started, but she'd disappeared into what Maggie assumed was the bedroom.

Maggie moved to the tree and examined the branches, fingering a tiny mouse ornament with delicate ears and a cheeky grin. "These are amazing."

He shrugged. "They're okay. I got better as I went."

She was awed by the craftsmanship but more by the whimsical nature of the figures. "You made these?"

"Don't sound so surprised. I'm a saddler, gotta be good with leather."

But the ornaments were more than well-crafted bits of leather, they were infused with a charm and sweetness she would not have expected.

"Used to have this mouse that took up residence in our pantry when we were kids. Helen was never scared of that thing. Had to talk her out of leaving it little cheese presents. She named it Lucy Lee."

She laughed. "Family name?"

Liam did not return the smile. "Mom's name."

There was such a depth of emotion in the two words, a flash of pain hidden in the navy depths of his eyes. She wanted to ask but did not dare and he did not offer so she sat in a richly upholstered armchair.

Liam removed his hat and put the wriggling dog on the floor. Jingles scampered over to Maggie. "Your dog is pigeon-toed," she said, scratching the animal behind the crooked ears until his doggie eyes rolled in pleasure.

"That's not the only thing cockeyed about this dog, believe me," Liam muttered. Hands on hips, he stared at the doorway, mouth working in thought. He was, she noticed again, an extremely handsome man.

And he probably knows it, she thought. Was

that why Liam and Tammy had not become anything permanent? Annoyed by her own thoughts, she straightened as Helen entered.

"Okay. Come on back," she said.

Once again, Liam deferred to Maggie, allowing her to pass him and enter the bedroom. It was another beautiful room, complete with a slender Christmas tree decorated all in silver, but Maggie had no eyes for any of it. All she could do was cry out and run to the pale woman lying in the bed, a bandage taped to her forehead.

"Tammy," she whispered, gathering her sister in her arms and trying to hide the tears.

Liam could only gape. When he summoned the wherewithal to close his mouth, he stared from Helen to the sniffling sisters and back again. "What…?" He stared. "I mean…why…?" He rubbed a palm over his beard-roughened chin when the words failed him again.

Helen raised an amused eyebrow. "Need a minute to formulate your question?"

"I'm circling around to it," he said, marshaling his thoughts.

Helen beat him to it. "You're probably wondering what Tammy is doing here."

"That is the question that rises to the top of

the list," he said as Maggie finally released her sister and they both wiped their eyes.

He found he was not distressed at the sight of his former girlfriend as much as completely befuddled.

Jingles, bored of the proceedings, leaped up onto the bed and nestled down next to Tammy. Liam was going to scold him severely when Maggie began to stroke the dog and Helen smiled adoringly at the mutt. He bit back his rebuke. Jingles had an uncanny ability to charm women. He wished he could do the same.

Tammy looked wan under the bandage on her temple, the fire missing in her words when she spoke. "Hi, Liam."

"Good to see you, Tammy," he said, politeness winning out temporarily over his aggravation.

She took a breath. "Helen took me in a few days ago. It was…" She cast a confused look at Helen.

"Wednesday night." Helen filled them in. "Actually she arrived just as I was talking to you that night on the phone. I recognized her and saw she was in trouble. Since there were no rooms, I put her up with me."

"And you didn't feel the need to tell me?" Liam asked, skewering Helen with a look.

"She asked me to keep her presence a secret

until she could talk to Maggie." Helen held up a hand to wave off his remark. "I know, Liam, you're cooking up a list of rebukes, but considering that things ended a little…awkwardly between you and Tammy, I figured it would be a kindness to both of you to keep it quiet until the situation was clearer."

He had no answer for that, but he felt the heat crawl up his neck. That wasn't all. He could see it in his sister's eyes, the shadow of guilt, the agony she still felt over the murder of her best friend, a tragedy for which she blamed herself. "I let her die," she'd told him one bitterly cold afternoon. "And now those babies have no mother." She'd steadfastly refused any consolation from him. It probably explained why she was so determined to step out on a limb for Tammy.

"Not a good idea to keep her here."

Helen's chin went up. "I'm not going to let her get hurt." He heard the unspoken, *Like I did with Fiona.*

He waited until Helen finally looked at him. "Honey, she's in deeper trouble than you know. She's got some guy after her."

Maggie nodded to her sister. "It must be Virgil, the one you warned me about. He almost killed me yesterday. I think he mistook me for you."

Tammy jerked. "Oh, Mags. Really?"

"I'm okay. Liam scared him off," Maggie said.

"Yeah, and I still got the pulled muscles to prove it." He stared at Tammy. "Who is this guy? And why didn't you turn this over to the cops if you're scared of him? Why put Maggie in danger?" His anger was stoked good and proper. All this lying, sneaking around… it wasn't right. And Tammy, it seemed, was the cause of it all. What really bothered him the most was that Helen hadn't looped him in. Helen had taken Tammy's side over his and the betrayal stung.

Now the old spark kindled in Tammy's expression. "His full name is Virgil Salvador and I would never have put my sister at risk, Liam, any more than you would knowingly put Helen in danger."

He wanted to stoke his anger, to add more fuel to his already simmering temper, but her sincerity drained him. It was the truth; he heard the twined cords of anger and regret deep down. "I do know that," he conceded, "but she's in danger anyway."

Tammy took Maggie's hand, knotting their fingers together. "If anything happened to you…" She gulped, blanching.

Maggie offered a bright smile. "I'm perfectly

fine, but why didn't you come to the lighthouse? Or call me at least?"

"My memory's messed up from the concussion. I was in a car accident. I think Virgil drove me off the road."

"What?" Liam and Maggie said at the same time.

She waved them off. "I'm okay, but I couldn't recall where I'd agreed to meet you and I'd lost my phone. I couldn't remember your number anyway.

"Things are coming back to me in bits and pieces. I woke up on Tuesday night in the hospital, after the wreck. That's when I messaged you, I think, to set up the meeting at the lighthouse. I snuck out and came here by taxi. I might have stopped on the way. I know I was at my trailer for a while. At least, I think that's what happened. It's all such a blur. My head was splitting, and I hurt my ankle, too. Somehow I wound up at the Lodge. Helen took me in. Gave me her bed, even."

Helen shrugged. "The sofa is perfectly comfy. She was sort of muddled, talking about jewelry or something, clearly exhausted, but she begged me not to call the police. I agreed to wait a few days. One of the Lodge guests is a doctor and he checked her out. He prescribed bed rest until the headaches die down and the ankle is less swollen. His opinion is that her confusion will lessen as time goes by."

Helen grinned. "And then I hear through the grapevine that Tammy Lofton is tootling around town. Neat trick, Maggie. I knew there had to be something odd going on if you were impersonating your sister. Nan at the Chuckwagon told me you and Liam were chatting in the parking lot. I felt it was time to get both sisters and my helpful brother in the same room and put our heads together. That's why I called you, Liam."

"Eventually," he reminded her. He tried to wrangle all the details into a cohesive picture. "Why is this Virgil guy after you, Tam?"

Tammy sucked in a breath and blew it out. "That part I do remember. Virgil moved in with his uncle Bill, the man I was tending to. Virgil's a bad man, greedy, and I suspected from the start he was out to steal from his uncle.

"Bill gets a little confused sometimes, and Virgil convinced him to buy a new car, which Virgil drives, a new cell phone…things like that. Bill owns a vintage diamond jewelry set that belonged to his wife, Elizabeth. She passed away a couple of months ago… Anyway, Virgil urged Bill to take out a hefty insurance policy on the jewelry. I heard him on the phone Tuesday—I don't know who with—saying he'd put the jewels out on the dresser and make sure Bill was asleep. He was arranging to have the jewelry stolen so Bill could claim the insurance money and Virgil could help himself to the settlement."

"Swell guy," Liam muttered.

"It was all happening right then. I immediately went to Bill, but I couldn't wake him. So I… I took the jewelry. I couldn't let Virgil steal it from Bill, not his wife's special things. It was an impulse. Stupid. I brought it to Driftwood and I left it with someone or hid it. At least, I think I did."

Maggie groaned. "But why not go straight to the police?"

"I was going to, but when I woke up in the hospital, I heard Virgil talking in the hallway and I panicked and headed to Driftwood. I figured I'd talk to Danny Patron at the police department, but he was not in. I got the jewelry hidden somewhere and I intended to call Joe, my boyfriend."

Liam resisted the urge to add, "The computer programmer."

"But I lost my phone, as I told you."

Maggie's mouth pinched. "At the lighthouse, Virgil told me if I didn't give him the jewelry, he would kill me."

Tammy clutched the blanket. "I'm scared for both of us. I just really want to talk to Joe." She waved a helpless hand. "Can you find him? He lives somewhere near Sand Dune and I know he's probably worried that I haven't called or texted him recently."

Liam tried for a patient tone. "One thing at a time. Police protection is the way to go."

"But Virgil will tell the police I stole the jewelry," Tammy cried. "Which I did, but they won't believe that I was trying to help. Virgil texted me right before the accident. He said he'd tell the cops that I'd been stealing from Bill all the while I was in his employ." She flushed crimson. "He said he'd paid off a pawnbroker to say I'd brought in several of Bill's possessions." She swallowed hard. "I'd never do that, but it looks so bad."

Liam didn't like the desperation he heard in her voice. "I know Danny Patron. He'll believe you and he'll give you a fair hearing."

Tammy started to cry. Liam shifted uncertainly. The situation was getting thicker than Aunt Ginny's pea soup. Jingles burrowed deeper into the blankets. Liam tried again. "You have to tell the police where the jewelry is, and Virgil will be off your back."

The room seemed to go ultra silent. The women all looked in the direction of the mantel where there was an antique clock Liam had given Helen for her twenty-first birthday. It must be chiming the hour. He could not hear it. He squashed the fear and turned back to Tammy. "Where'd you hide the jewelry? Or who did you leave it with?"

"That's the problem," Tammy said. "I can't remember."

SIX

"Can't remember?" Maggie tried to process.

Liam blew out a breath. "Okay. We can figure this out." He turned to Helen. "Did she tell you where she'd been when she arrived here?"

"No, not really anything specific, but it was frantic here and the lobby was hopping with holiday check-ins. I didn't get a chance to pay full attention until later when I got her upstairs, but she was so tired and miserable, I put her straight to bed." She patted Tammy's knee. "I'm sorry, honey, but I don't know where you were between your hospital stay and when you showed up here."

"Maybe you slept in your car or on someone's sofa. I'll ask your neighbors at the trailer park if you mentioned anything." Maggie jotted notes in her phone, making a list of all the names Tammy spooled out, everyone she considered a friend in Driftwood.

Helen started, took a phone from her pocket

and read the message. "I'm sorry, I have to go. Chef needs help."

Maggie wished for a lightning-quick moment that she could go, too, lose herself in the business of a restaurant kitchen, dissolve her concern in clouds of sizzling butter and boiling pots of pasta. Missing jewelry even in a small town like Driftwood was a needle in the proverbial haystack.

Helen kissed Tammy and headed for the door. "You just call me on the house phone if you need me."

Liam called to Helen, "Gonna need to finish this conversation, sis."

"Yes, Liam. I know I will not get out of the scolding you intend to give me." She kissed him on the cheek and breezed out.

Tammy stared with wide eyes. "I don't know what to do."

Maggie straightened. "I do. I'll be you for a while, until you're better. I'm going to snoop around town and try to figure out who you left the jewelry with, then we'll take it to the police, just like you intended."

"But I can't remember…"

"I'm sure you'll get your memory back, but in the meantime, I'll ask around, at the Chuckwagon, too. I'm sure you made friends there."

She shot a quick glance at her watch. "I'm late getting back right now."

"In the meantime…" Liam broke in in such a severe manner that Jingles looked up from his stupor, startled. "Virgil Salvador is still out there, looking to either get his jewelry back or to hurt you both."

Tammy shuddered. "I won't let you risk yourself for me, Mags. I won't."

"I owe you one, remember?"

"That was a long time ago," Tammy said. "The debt, if there ever was any, has been repaid a zillion times over."

Maggie shook her head. "I would not be here if it wasn't for you." She took in Liam's curiosity. "There was a restaurant fire. She got me out."

"You'd have done the same for me." Tears leaked down her sister's cheeks.

"No crying," Maggie said. "I've got the list of everyone you remember talking to. Just keep trying to think if there's anyone else."

"But Joe…how can I warn him?"

"I'll ask my brother to help track him down. Mitch is a retired US marshal." Liam held up a hand. "Don't worry. He'll keep it on the down low." His face went stone-still. "But this half-baked investigation plan is not going to work. Don't you remember how close Virgil got yesterday?"

"This is a private family issue, Liam," Maggie said.

"Not anymore it's not," he half growled.

She stood, catching his ferocious gaze with her own. "Thanks for your help, but I'll take it from here."

His lips twitched. A silent rebuff.

"Not gonna let you do this alone," he said finally.

She tipped her chin up. "I don't need your permission."

"Oh, boy," Tammy muttered. "It's like a Western standoff. Where are the tumbleweeds rolling by?"

Liam started to speak, then stopped. Finally he crammed his hat on his head.

"That's where you're wrong," Liam said to Maggie. "You and Tammy drew my sister into this mess and that means it's a twofer. If you get Helen, you earn yourself her ornery bear of a brother, too."

"I said I don't need your help." Maggie's tone was more strident this time, so clear even this mountain of a cowboy could not misunderstand.

"I gotta go." Liam whistled for the dog who jumped off the bed and bounded over so fast he skidded on the hardwood and sailed right into Liam's shins.

Maggie relaxed a fraction as he backed off

until he shook his head. "No offense, ma'am, but you're gettin' my help whether you think you need it or not." He about-faced and stalked out the door, Jingles following merrily behind.

Maggie blew out a breath.

"What did you ever see in him?" she asked her sister.

Tammy laughed. "He grows on a person and you'd better watch out, Maggie, because he only badgers people he takes an interest in."

Maggie kissed her sister and left, being sure to go slow enough that she would not run into Liam. She figured by the time she finished unloading the pies from the van, he would be long gone.

People he takes an interest in?

Why did that thought sparkle around her like the glimmering lights on the Christmas tree?

Liam spoke to Mitch right away, asking him to find Joe. "Last name of Albertson." Mitch had spent years in the US Marshals office tracking the most desperate and degenerate fugitives in the world, so he was sure locating Joe would be a piece of cake.

Mitch did not press him for details, but Liam could see the questions nestled deep in his brother's black eyes. "I promise I'll tell you everything when I can."

Mitch nodded but didn't look convinced about Liam's judgment. Liam wasn't so sure about his own wisdom, either.

When he finished the conversation, he rode out with Chad to tinker with a watering system that was not up to par and then replaced a flat tire on one of the ranch tractors.

Skipping lunch, he got down to business in the workhouse, attending to some accumulated tack repairs that had been piling up on his workbench. He eyed the small piece of skirt he'd cut with the hydraulic press, waiting there on the saddle tree. He was making a child-size saddle to give to Charlie for Christmas. The seat he'd cut by hand with a head knife, custom fitting the saddle for both Charlie and Sugar, the horse Charlie would be riding. Though he longed to work on it, he was far too distracted.

He had called over to the Chuckwagon twice and heard that Maggie was still waiting tables and helping in the kitchen. Her shift ended at five, he'd found out from Nan, and he intended to ensure he was there when she clocked out, no matter how she felt about it. His thoughts alternately pinballed between irritation, aggravation and, oddly, fascination. The latter he could not understand so he did his best to stow it somewhere deep down.

Chad popped his head into Liam's workshop, a worried frown on his face.

Liam snapped to attention, putting down the tack. "What's wrong?"

"Aunt Ginny's fallen. Got her up and on the sofa, but she won't go to the doc."

"Uncle Gus can't make her?"

"He's away getting lumber in town. I left a message on his cell. He doesn't pick up when he's driving."

Liam didn't need to hear any more. He hurried to the house to find Aunt Ginny looking more peeved than pained, sitting on the sofa with her foot propped on a Christmas-patterned throw pillow. "I'm right as rain," she said. "I just missed the last few steps of the ladder. You didn't need to get Liam, Chad."

"Aw-ww there's no place I'd rather be than with you, Aunt Ginny," Liam drawled. "You're my best gal."

She rolled her eyes.

"Let me just take a look at that ankle, huh?" Liam had served as a medical sergeant among other duties in his Green Beret career. He palpated her joint and sent Chad for an ice pack. "Don't think it's broken…"

"There, you see—" she started.

"But I recommend we take you into town for an X-ray."

Her brows drew together. "A recommendation from one of my boys is something I can choose to ignore."

"Not advisable, Aunt Ginny."

"I'm not going."

"Yes, you are," Uncle Gus said, striding through the door and hurrying to her side. He knelt next to the sofa. "Got your message, Chad, and I'm taking her right now to the emergency."

"I do not need a doctor," Ginny snapped.

He cupped a hand behind his ear. "Hear that, Ginny? It's the sound of me putting my foot down."

She allowed a grudging smile that turned into a girlish giggle. "I didn't recognize that sound."

"That's because I don't do it very often, not where my lady is concerned." He lifted her off the sofa.

"I don't need carrying," she said.

"Not losing a chance to hold a gorgeous gal in my arms," Gus said. "Quiet down now and cooperate, my love."

Liam went ahead to open doors and they got Aunt Ginny installed in the passenger seat of Uncle Gus's truck and on their way to the hospital. Liam's heart squeezed with the tenderness between the two. A love like theirs was a precious thing indeed. An image of Maggie flashed in his brain, but he shook it promptly away. Hunger was messing with his mind, had to be.

His cell phone read a few minutes to five, almost Maggie's quitting time. "Gotta go," he called to Chad.

He drove as quickly as he could to the Chuckwagon, relieved to see the Corvette still in the back lot.

The restaurant smelled of the cook's renowned chili and corn bread, which made Liam's stomach rumble. He wished he'd grabbed a slice of Aunt Ginny's holiday loaf before he'd left. He had no idea what the little red and green flecks were that dotted the loaves and he didn't care. Delicious, was all he needed to know.

Ignoring his hunger, Liam scanned the booths and tables without spotting Maggie. He let himself into the kitchen. Tiny, the enormous cook with a blaze of red hair atop his freckled face, stood over the commercial range, cheeks flushed from the heat.

"Whatcha want, Liam? You looking for one of my special grilled cheese right out of the pan? A side of caramelized onions? I'll hook you up."

Liam grinned. "No, sir, though your grilled cheese sandwiches are a wonder to behold. Looking for Mag—I mean Tammy Lofton."

Tiny flipped a bunch of onions over, loosing a cloud of steam into the air. "Dunno what happened to that gal, but she learned to cook since I seen her last. She's a wonder."

"Where is she?"

Liam didn't catch Tiny's reply, so he repeated the question.

"Left," Tiny said.

"But her car's in the lot."

"Nan told her to take the Chuckwagon van. They loaded up the apple muffins we baked tonight to deliver to the Veteran's Hall first thing in the morning for the parade planners."

He was already turning to go, waving a thank-you to Tiny before he'd finished flipping the onions one more time. *No reason to worry,* Liam thought, *she's probably fine.* Except that the Corvette in the parking lot was like a blaring advertisement for Virgil if he was still in town.

Come find me here, it screamed. But maybe Virgil realized that Maggie had an ally now. Maybe he'd moved on.

And maybe Liam was going to wake up one morning and have his hearing restored and a million bucks in his pocket.

Not gonna happen.

He took the road to the trailer park as fast as he dared.

She's okay, he told himself, surprised at his own need to believe it. Did he feel such intensity because of how he'd thought he'd felt about

Tammy? Was his determination to ensure her sister's safety coming from that?

Though he gripped the steering wheel and tried for calm, his pulse continued to accelerate.

Coming, Maggie.

SEVEN

The winter sunset bathed the road in golden glory as Maggie drove the rattling van to Tammy's trailer. She'd picked up a possible lead from her hectic day at the Chuckwagon, a name that she'd also gotten from Tammy's garbled memory. A woman named Yoriko, an artist who lived near the beach.

Lost in her thoughts, Maggie finally noticed that the gas gauge in the old van was almost on empty. With a sigh, she turned into the impeccably neat station and fueled up. A man with wire-rimmed glasses and a swoop of sandy hair pulled in behind her. All of a sudden Maggie became acutely aware of how dark the night was, how lonely the empty gas station felt. She hadn't seen Virgil clearly at the lighthouse. Could the unobtrusive man be him?

She tried to spy on him beneath the brim of her Chuckwagon baseball cap, but she couldn't get a good look. She felt his eyes on her. Maggie hurriedly collected the credit card receipt and got back into the driver's seat. It was almost completely dark as she left the station. The man with the glasses looked up as she drove by, giving her a friendly salute, but his gaze lingered on her for a moment too long.

Friendly? Or a friend of Virgil's?

Was she being pragmatic or paranoid?

After a couple of miles, when his car did not appear in her rearview mirror, she relaxed a fraction.

Rolling into the trailer park, she noticed the nearest trailer to hers, a good hundred yards off, was dark, with a vacant look about it. Tammy's was at the end of the row, near a thick cluster of oak trees standing in a cushion of tall grasses. The click of some concealed insect and the rustling of leaves were the only sounds as she exited the van. Shrugging off the prickle of unease, she strode, keys ready, to the trailer door. As she started to slide the key in, the door creaked open.

A glance told her the story. Furniture was turned over, cushions scattered on the floor with the stuffing ripped out. In the kitchen, the cupboards were open, their contents disgorged onto the worn linoleum floor.

Breath caught, she backed down the steps and rushed to the van, pulling her phone from her pocket. Whom should she call? Liam? Should she break her promise to Tammy and phone the police?

Just get away from here and decide.

She reached for the door handle when she felt a presence behind her. Whirling around, she found a man standing close, very close.

"Hello, Tammy," Virgil said, the accent unmistakable.

The scream died in her throat as her back impacted the cold steel of the van behind her. He was dressed in dark slacks and a soft polo shirt, leather boots on his feet, hands gloved.

"You stay away from me," she breathed.

He looked perplexed. "I came to talk to you. Talk, that's all." He waved a hand at the trailer. "I found your trailer door open, so I looked inside. It's a mess. I figured I'd stay because you need my help. You've made an enemy out of someone, obviously."

Liar. "Don't patronize me. You tossed the trailer, Virgil, and if you don't get away from me, I'm going to start screaming."

He quirked an eyebrow. "I want my jewelry back."

"It's not your jewelry, it's Bill Salvador's."

Virgil nodded. "Of course. He's really quite upset about the whole thing. I mean, he trusted you, believed in you, and he doesn't want to think you're a thief."

"I'm not. I took the jewelry to keep it safe."

He shrugged. "When I show him the security tape…"

"Go ahead," she said, forcing courage she did not feel. "As a matter of fact, let's go to the police, too, now. I'll tell them everything I know about you."

"That isn't a good option right now." He straightened, his gelled hair glinting in the starlight. "I have to get this resolved quickly. I…" He cocked his head. "I have a commitment that requires me to have the jewelry back."

"I hid it," she blurted. "Someplace you'll never find it."

"Then you'll have to bring it to me, Tammy. Quickly."

Tell him you'll get it. Make up a story. Anything to get him away.

"I…"

He raised a hand. She flinched, but he did not touch her. Instead his fingers stopped before they skimmed her face. "It's the perfume," he said.

"What?"

"Your perfume. You're not wearing perfume. Why? You always wear that floral scent."

She fought for control as he leaned closer,

close enough that she could feel his warm breath on her cheek.

"I'm very in tune with you, Tammy. I know what kind of tea you drink, apple cinnamon, and the type of hand lotion you use, the lilac and shea butter."

Her skin crawled.

"I find women appreciate it when you notice important details." He smiled.

"Get away from me."

When he didn't retreat, she opened her mouth to scream but he fell back a step and pressed a gloved finger to his lips.

"Tammy," he whispered. "There's something different about you. We were friends, weren't we? I convinced my uncle to hire you, didn't I? I don't understand why you're being so obstinate."

Now she edged away. A few more inches and she'd be out of arm's reach. *Run back to the trailer? Scream for help?*

He slid a hand into his jacket pocket and her lungs quit working.

"It's almost like you're not the same Tammy," he murmured. "But how could that be? You wouldn't be lying to me, would you? I can't stand liars—"

He had not finished the last syllable when she lunged away into the darkness.

* * *

Liam took the graveled road into the trailer park and slowed to the requisite five miles an hour, fighting himself to hold to it. He opened the window to let in a rush of cold air, dangling his arm into the night. For some reason it always calmed him to be able to feel the movement of the air. Here along the coast it was clean, pure, and his lungs craved it as much as when he'd been deployed to the desert.

He hit the brakes as a blur of white collided with his driver's-side door.

Maggie's outstretched palm impacted the metal, her eyes wide with shock, lips open as if in a scream.

He jammed the truck into Park and leaped out, wrapping her in his arms, her fear a palpable current. "Maggie, what is it?"

She said something he couldn't hear. He pulled away and looked into her face, his fingers framing her cheeks. "Tell me again."

"He's here. Virgil," she mumbled. "I got away."

Something hardened like quick-drying cement in his gut. "Get in the truck and stay there," he ground out through gritted teeth. Grabbing his rifle, he ran toward her trailer. He thought she'd said something, but he didn't catch it.

Her trailer was quiet, the door ajar, so he crept

inside, checking the rooms and closets. No Virgil. Outside again, he walked the whole perimeter of the structure with no sign of the guy until he saw the flattened track of mashed grass leading off into the trees.

Torso bent low, he followed the trail into the dripping woods. He listened, straining his good ear to its limit, but he caught no clues as to Virgil's whereabouts. Before his hearing loss, the insects would have told him, their sudden silence indicating they'd been unsettled by an intruder. Now he was without any aid until he caught the flicker of taillights on the far end of the woods. Virgil had parked far enough away that he could approach undetected. The car drove off and Liam's spirits plunged.

Muttering to himself, he retraced his steps to the truck where Tammy sat, shivering, arms wrapped around herself.

He got in next to her, realizing that he'd probably left her too hastily. "I'm sorry. I should have made sure you were okay before I bolted and left you alone."

"I'm okay," she said. "But the trailer is ripped apart inside."

"I noticed. I figured it was either Virgil or you're a terrible housekeeper."

She didn't smile. "He said it wasn't him. He said…" She began to tremble harder.

He took her hand and squeezed. Her fingers were so cold that he instinctively pressed them between his palms, enjoying the strength there, hands that were used to hard work, but so much more delicate than his own calloused paws. "Police?"

"Not until I talk to Tammy."

"They should see it, process any evidence."

"I doubt there is any. He was wearing gloves." He sighed. "But…"

"I'm going back inside to check again for the jewelry. Maybe it really is in there and Virgil missed it, too. That's why he scared me. I have to find it, for Tammy's sake. I pretended I knew where it was, but I don't know if Virgil believed me."

Liam bit back another attempt to persuade her to loop in the police. "Let's go inside, then. Assess the damage, get you something warm to drink first and then you can tell me everything."

Without giving her time to argue, he put the truck in Drive and parked it near the trailer. She even allowed him enough time to shimmy around and open the passenger door for her. That wasn't a good sign. Snaking his arm along her shoulders, he felt the shudders like electric shocks coursing through her petite frame. Anger rattled his insides.

Never, ever, disrespect a woman. It was one

thing he'd learned from his dad. It probably explained why his father had sunk into an impenetrable abyss after he'd wrecked the car and killed Liam's mother. It did not explain, not to Liam, why Richard Pike had wrecked his children's lives, as well. Weren't they worth trying for? Fighting against the tide of depression that made him throw away his own life as well as theirs? There was no profit in saddling up that old horse at the present.

Inside the trailer, he closed the door and louvered shut the blinds before taking a series of pictures. He figured since he'd been in the trailer previously, sharing a few meals with Tammy, his fingerprints were already present, so he wasn't messing up any potential Virgil prints if the man had somehow decided to remove his gloves. Shoving aside a flattened fake plant, he set a cushion back onto the sofa and settled her on it. Up-righting a chair as he went, he entered the kitchen, located a mug that hadn't been smashed and filled it with water from the tap. Though the microwave door was open, the unit hadn't been damaged, so he zapped the water, snagged a tea bag from the littered tile counter, plunked it in and brought it to her.

She wrapped her palms around it. "Thank you."

"You're welcome. Tea is the only thing I know

how to cook, so now you've experienced the entire Liam Pike menu." A tiny smile quirked her mouth as she sipped. He grabbed the chair, straddled it and waited, as patiently as he knew how, until she was ready to talk. The story came out in fits and starts.

"So he needs the jewelry right away, huh?" Liam said after she finished. "It's not enough to claim the insurance money for Bill so he can steal it, and frame Tammy for the jewelry theft?"

She stared without really seeing him. "He needs it for 'some other commitment' he said. And he…"

Liam leaned forward. "What?"

"He noticed I wasn't wearing Tammy's perfume. He knows all kinds of personal details about her. It was creepy." She looked at him. "Let go."

"Of what?"

"The chair. You're going to break it."

He realized he had the back of the chair in a stranglehold that was making the wood creak. He eased off. "I don't like hearing he was that close to you." Had that come off as too protective? Probably, judging by the look on her face, but it was true. The thought that Virgil Salvador had been within inches of Maggie made him want to hog-tie the guy. Not to mention the fact that he'd obviously been way too attentive to Tammy, as well. But Tammy knew how to handle obnoxious men; he'd never seen her intimidated by anyone male or female until recently. Maggie was a softer, gentler woman than her sister, he somehow knew. A woman who stirred up his protective streak. He forced his brain to focus. "He didn't find the jewelry here."

"No, but he found me." She swallowed, the movement visible in her graceful throat.

When he reached for her, she stood. "I'm going to look again."

"Okay. I'll help."

They searched for well over an hour. He stuck to the kitchen and common areas, leaving the bedroom for her. They met back in the kitchen with nothing to show for their efforts but a five dollar bill from under the sofa and a spare trailer key fallen into the crack between the sink and the cupboards.

He squared his shoulders and fired off another round of good, common sense. "All right. It's two to zip now, and he's won both rounds here and at the lighthouse. We should go to the police."

She sighed and, to his great surprise, nodded. "I think you're right. If he can get to me so easily, it will only be a matter of time before he discovers I'm not Tammy. I need to talk to Tammy first. You said you trust Danny Patron?"

"I do."

"Tammy does, too, to some degree. I think it's why she came here to Driftwood in the first place instead of going to the cops in Sand Dune."

"Danny's a good man. You won't be sorry. I'll drive you right after you pack up a bundle."

She raised an eyebrow. "A bundle of what?"

He pushed the kitchen chair in. "Clothes and whatever you need to borrow from your sister. You can't stay here."

"I don't have anywhere else to go. It will be fine once I…"

"Since the Lodge is booked, you can stay in the saddlery at Roughwater Ranch." He kept his attention on the messy trailer floor. "There's a little room with a bed and a tiny bathroom. Kinda rustic, but it'll do. I can even loan you a ridiculous excuse for a dog." He stopped and looked at her. "Well? Shouldn't you be getting a move on?"

"You're bossing me."

"Aw, not bossing, motivating."

She stared at him for a long moment and then the autumn hues of her eyes lit with a gleam of amusement. "Is that what they call it where you're from?"

"Yes, ma'am, by practically everyone."

He couldn't hear her laugh, but he guessed it was small and silvery.

What is the matter with you, Liam? She's Tammy's sister, remember?

Just helping out, was all.

Motivating, he told himself as he waited for her.

EIGHT

Liam ushered Maggie into the passenger seat, promising to bring Chad later to retrieve the van. She wished he wouldn't do that. Use such impeccable manners. It made her all uneasy and fluttery inside to have his supporting hand under her elbow…the way he pulled the seat belt over for her. She was strong and capable and didn't need such assistance. At the same time, she could not deny that Liam's presence drove some of the uncertainty away.

When she called the Lodge, Helen told them that Tammy had been given some pain medicine for her ankle and was fast asleep. There would be no discussing the police involvement with her until morning. The fact didn't discourage Liam in the least.

"First thing tomorrow, then. Aunt Ginny is home from the ER with her ankle taped, so Jane's cooking. That's my brother's new wife."

"Your brother?"

"In every way except the DNA. Chad, too. Mitch and Chad are brothers to me and Helen." He chuckled. "Now we got ourselves a sister in Jane and I got promoted to uncle to her little son Charlie. He's almost four. Cracks me up how much he loves trains. Same way I felt about toy soldiers when I was his age."

"So you were soldier material as a kid, too?"

He jerked a look at her. "Nah."

"Why did you become a Green Beret?"

He grinned. "Doesn't everyone want to be the best of the best?"

"No, so why did you?"

He shifted, fiddling with the buttons on the heater. "Haven't been asked that in a long while."

She waited patiently.

He huffed out a breath. "Uh, my dad sort of checked out of our lives after my mom died. This one time…" He rubbed at his brow. "I was around fifteen, I think. I have this vivid memory of him breaking down at the Vietnam Veterans Memorial because those were his buddies, his family. I felt this strange mixture of pride and resentment. He'd been something, mattered in some way, and he had this family that meant more to him than we did. I guess I…" He shifted again. "Wanted something like that, too."

"You're so close to Helen."

"What?"

He hadn't heard. "You have such a tight bond with Helen," she said a bit louder. "I assumed you were from a pretty close family."

"Helen probably would like me to be a little less bonded. She says I act like I'm the boss of her."

It was hard for Maggie to make out the subtle shift of his demeanor, but she heard it in his tone, the forced lightness, the cheerful patina that covered up something much deeper. He was sorry he'd shared things about his father with her, she surmised.

He parked the truck in the curving driveway of a stunning two-story ranch-style home with an elegant tower rising above the top floor. "Let's get some dinner. I'm starved."

He'd dismissed their moment of intimacy firmly. Unsure why she felt stung by his reaction, she followed him into the main house, through the tiled foyer and into a warm, inviting dining room done in varying types of wood.

A dark-haired woman with her hair pulled into a ponytail was just sliding a tureen of corn chowder onto a festive table. Behind her was an enormous man, even taller than Liam, with a scar on his cheek, dark hair and eyes.

"Mitch Whitehorse," he said, dwarfing her hand in his. "And this is my wife, Jane, and our son, Charlie." *Our son.* She heard a mountain of pride in those words, though she knew that Charlie was not Mitch's biological child.

He shot a look at Liam. "Got the photos of the trailer you sent to me and Danny Patron, but I'm not certain why you didn't share the situation earlier. You have a few things to explain."

"Yes," Liam said. "I do."

Charlie was staring in rapt attention at the train track circling the base of a twinkling tree.

"Gonna say hello to your uncle?" Liam snatched up the boy and swung him onto his shoulders. Charlie squealed in delight, gripping Liam's ears as he carried him to the table. "This is Miss Maggie," Liam said. "You met her sister Tammy. They look a lot alike."

Charlie solemnly reached down from his perch and shook her hand. "Mice to meet you."

"Nice," Liam said with a laugh, "not mice."

Maggie marveled at the joy that shone from Liam's face as he lifted his nephew down and settled him in a chair.

Charlie frowned in concentration as he bent his fingers and thrust them toward Liam.

"Whatcha doin', kiddo?" Liam asked.

"He's showing you what he learned in preschool," Jane said.

Liam's expression was perplexed so she explained. "It's sign language for 'I love you.'"

Liam's mouth softened, splitting into a tender grin as he bent to kiss Charlie. "I love you, too," Maggie heard him whisper.

Charlie beamed. Her heart throbbed at the tender moment between the two.

"Your mama's made something yummy," Liam said conspiratorially. "We're gonna have a good meal."

"You'd eat cardboard if we served it to you," Jane said.

Liam pulled out the chair for Maggie to sit. She blushed. Dinner was usually a bowl of soup eaten standing up between shifts. This grand table with the centerpiece of poinsettias and woven striped napkins dazzled her.

The woman who must be Aunt Ginny, silvered hair cut in a neat pixie and her ankle in a brace, arrived, followed by a handsome man in his sixties.

"I'm Gus and this is Ginny. Welcome." He shook his head. "Forgive my staring. Liam filled me in just a little. We met your sister when she and Liam were…" He cleared his throat. "Well, anyway, you just look so much alike I would have mistaken you for your sister in a heartbeat."

"It's the twin thing," she said. "But I'm younger by two minutes."

Everyone laughed. After Uncle Gus said

grace, they dug into the savory soup and hunks of homemade herb bread. Maggie didn't realize how hungry she'd been. Liam ate heartily, also, reaching over to butter the bread for Charlie and wipe the dribbled milk from the boy's chin. The simple gesture fluttered something inside her chest.

When the meal was almost finished, Liam gave a streamlined version of Maggie and Tammy's situation. "Maggie's staying in the saddlery tonight, Ginny and Gus are okay with it. We're going to lay this all out for Danny Patron tomorrow. I already called and left a message on his cell phone, and we're driving over there to meet with him as soon as she talks to her sister."

Mitch fingered his water glass. "Need me on this?"

"I was hoping I could rope you in."

"No need for roping. I'll be there." Mitch didn't smile but his gaze came to rest on Maggie. "Liam's good at recruiting help."

"Green Berets are force multipliers," he said with a grin. "That's one of our strengths. We go into hostile territory and win over the hearts and minds of the people."

"Candy diplomacy," Mitch said with a smile. "Your best trick is winning over the stomachs of the people."

Liam laughed. "Whatever works."

Charlie was excused to watch the train go around the tree.

"I apologize for bringing our problems into your home," Maggie said.

Jane waited until Charlie was engrossed before she said softly, "I felt the same way not too long ago." She looked at her husband. "This family saved me and Charlie and gave us back our future. We would do anything for Liam—" her gaze shifted to Maggie "—and anyone he cared about."

Maggie found she was not able to meet Jane's eyes. *Cared about? Her?* She immediately felt the sting of her own foolishness. Jane obviously meant that the family was willing to help because of Liam's connection with Tammy.

Mitch cleared his throat. "Checked out Joe Albertson. He's clean. He was hired to write a computer program for Bill Salvador's feed and grain business. He's got a good rep for quality work. Lives in an apartment outside of Sand Dune. Drives a five-year-old Subaru. No priors except for a speeding ticket and a fender bender."

Liam nodded. "You work fast."

"I work smart. I texted you his phone number so you can pass it on to Tammy." His eyes swiveled to Maggie. "If Virgil is able to get close to you, it's a matter of time before he finds your sister, too."

"I'm not going to let that happen," Liam said.

Maggie pursed her lips. "I appreciate it, really, but we don't expect ongoing help. There's no reason to put you out any further. I know Virgil's dangerous and I'm way out of my depth here, but I will do what I have to for my sister."

Mitch nodded after a moment. "I get it. Same applies to me and mine." He reached for Jane's hand and kissed her on the knuckles. "Sometimes you have to take risks to protect what's important."

Maggie felt Liam looking at her and dropped her gaze to her lap. Relieved when everyone began to clear the plates from the table, Maggie gathered up an armful.

"Hey, now. Let me help," Liam said.

"I got this. You're a force multiplier, I'm a restaurant rock star. Go play with Charlie."

That made him tip back his head and laugh with gusto. The sound thrilled her. Before she could react, he leaned over and kissed her temple as if it was the most natural thing in the world, the brush of his warm mouth buzzing her pulse. Then he was gone. But the off-kilter cascade of emotions remained.

Temporary situation, she told herself. Liam Pike, her sister's ex-boyfriend, was not going to become a stalwart presence in her life. Exes were and would always be off-limits. Period.

He's just a charming cowboy helper, she mused, but the words failed to quell the hum dancing deep in her veins.

Liam brought out the box he'd stowed away on a bookshelf, opening it up for Charlie.

The boy's eyes widened to the size of silver dollars as he took out the wooden tunnel. Liam had asked Mitch to carve it and then Liam had painted it with snowy mountains and added a minuscule mountain goat wearing a collar of jingle bells.

"I thought that was going to be a Christmas present," Mitch said.

"Nah, I'm working on something else for his real Christmas present."

"You're going to spoil him."

"That's what uncles are for."

Something crossed Mitch's face and his mouth tightened. Liam waited.

"It's hard to forget that his biological father is…"

A serial killer.

"Behind bars, so he loses his kin badge," Liam said firmly. "Mitch, God is good and Charlie's got an amazing father in you and a spectacular uncle in me, if we're being honest."

Mitch fired him an uncertain smile. "Sometimes I can't believe it."

"Believe it. Everyone will confirm that I'm spectacular."

He got the laugh he'd earned. Mitch stepped away to answer his cell and Liam knelt next to the train tracks that circled the tree, helping Charlie set the tunnel in place. They both cheered when the toy train chugged around and emerged from the newly installed tunnel.

He stood and backed away a step or two, holding his cell phone to get a picture of Charlie and the train. A presence made him jerk around to find Maggie behind him. His elbow knocked the mug of cocoa she held, spilling it all down her front.

"Oh, man," he said, rushing to the table and grabbing up some napkins. He stood there, face burning, helplessly clutching napkins. "I didn't hear you. I'm awful sorry."

"It's okay." With a calm smile, she took the napkins from him while he grabbed the half-empty mug from her. She dabbed at the splatters on her shirt and pants. "I've been showered with plenty worse stuff, let me tell you. You haven't lived until you've had liver and onions all down your front."

He tried to smile but something thick and

heavy held down his spirit. He hadn't heard her. "Did I… I mean…are you burned?"

"No, it wasn't that hot."

But it could have been and it might just have showered down upon Charlie and scalded him. Liam shook his head, eyes on his boots, and then felt her arm on his.

"It's okay. An accident. No harm done."

No harm, except another reminder of his narrowing world. He forced a smile. "Hey, yeah. Well, I hope you didn't have your heart set on that cocoa."

"It was for Charlie, but no worries. I'll make him another cup. Do you want some, too?"

"No, uh, I'm just gonna make sure the cabin is all set for you." He turned, but she sidled in front of him.

"I'll go, too. You shouldn't do all the work."

"Nah," he said, forcing a jolly tone. "Easier on my own."

He hurried to the door, ready to step into the darkness that would allow him to hide his feelings. As he reached for the handle, the doorbell chimed.

Yanking it open, Liam found a stranger with thick, sandy hair and wire-rimmed glasses standing on the porch. His guard went up. Strangers didn't usually invite themselves onto ranch property, not unless there was a very good reason.

"Can I help you?" Liam said.

"Yes," the man said. His gaze drifted past Liam. A quick glance told Liam that his object was Maggie. He saw her expression change from confusion to recognition to the barest flicker of fear.

Liam edged over a step, blocking the man's view. "I said, can I help you?"

The man nodded. "I'm sure you can," he said, looking at Maggie. "I have been looking all over the place for you, Tammy."

NINE

Maggie, steeling her jittering nerves, came to the door, determined that Liam would not assign himself the role of her personal bodyguard.

"I didn't get a name," Liam growled.

"Joe," he said, looking from Liam to Maggie in confusion. "Tammy, what's wrong? Don't you recognize me? I've been looking all over for you. I just got your text, but it wasn't from your phone and you didn't tell me exactly where you were, just in Driftwood somewhere. I was so worried when you said something about taking some jewelry. I…"

Joe. Tammy's boyfriend. She'd messaged him from Helen's cell phone, no doubt. "I saw you at the gas station, didn't I?"

"Yes, I thought it was you, but I couldn't tell in the dark and I couldn't figure out why you'd be driving that van. Tam…what's wrong? Why are you here now?" He looked at Liam and his eyes narrowed. "Wait a minute. Is this your cowboy ex-boyfriend?" His face hardened. "And you came back for *his* help? What does he know about anything?"

"More than a computer programmer does," Liam fired back.

Joe's brown eyes flashed.

Maggie stepped forward. "Joe, listen. I need to explain some things. Please."

Liam grudgingly stepped aside to allow Joe to pass into the entry. He immediately folded Maggie into a hug and she stiffened.

"It's okay, baby. I'll take care of you," Joe said. "I'm not going to let Virgil hurt you."

"Hey—" Liam started reaching for Joe, but Maggie was already detaching herself.

"I'm not Tammy," she said.

"What?" Joe gaped.

Liam shot her a questioning look. She ignored him. Yes, she could impersonate Tammy around town, but there was no way she was willing or able to pretend to be Joe's girlfriend.

"I'm her twin sister, Maggie."

"Twins." Understanding dawned in his eyes. "Right. You— I mean Tammy told me that." Joe rocked back on his heels. "What in the world is going on here?"

"Virgil drove Tammy off the road when she was on her way back to Sand Dune to get you. Virgil is after her, but she can't remember where she hid the jewelry because she's got a head injury."

He frowned. "I can't believe this."

Maggie nodded. "I'm pretending to be Tammy to find the jewelry and keep him away from her."

Joe grabbed his head with his hands. "This is nuts. Tammy said she took the jewelry to prevent it being stolen?"

"By Virgil to fake the insurance claim so he could weasel the money away from Bill Salvador."

Liam folded his arms across his chest. "You work for Bill, too. You must know what Virgil is like."

"How did you know I worked for him?"

Liam shrugged. "Cowboys know everything."

Joe glared. "This isn't a joke."

"I know it," Liam snapped. "Better than you do."

Maggie stepped between them. "We're going to the police tomorrow, first thing."

"But when you messaged… I mean when Tammy did, she said we had to steer clear of the cops."

"Things have changed," Liam said. "Too many threats. It's the best decision."

"According to you?" Joe countered.

Maggie blew out a breath. She felt like she

was standing between two alpha bulls. "Joe, I can't risk my safety or Tammy's. It's for the best. Danny Patron is a cop we can trust."

He was silent a moment. "Where's Tammy? I want to see her. Is she here? She hasn't returned my texts."

Liam shook his head, lips tight. She knew what he was thinking. No one should know where Tammy was hiding, even a man claiming to be her boyfriend.

"Uh…she's safe, Joe, probably sleeping, and she's borrowed a phone, which is why you didn't recognize the number. That's all I can tell you right now."

Joe's jaw clenched. "I see. I'm not to be trusted with Tammy's whereabouts?"

"I'll tell her you're here," Maggie said soothingly. "Give me your phone number and we can arrange a meeting."

She handed Joe her cell phone and he punched in his number.

Maggie noted his hands were trembling with suppressed anger. "I'm sorry, I don't mean to offend you, but I've never met you before and someone has almost killed me thinking I was Tammy."

He blanched slightly. "Virgil? I can't say I'm completely surprised. He lives to feed his greed, and he'll never satisfy that appetite."

"What do you know about him exactly?"

Joe glared right at Liam. "I know he's bad and I know I'm going to keep Tammy safe from him if it's the last thing I do even without your co-operation." He whirled on his heel and marched back to his car, the engine roaring away into the darkness.

Liam locked the door. "High-strung dude."

"He's worried about her, and you were rude."

"Don't care. Never met the guy. Not gonna trust him until I know him."

"Tammy will want to see him as soon as possible."

"After we talk to the cops. I'll feel better when we've got everyone on notice that law enforcement is on board." Liam's coppery brows drew together. "Joe might help get to the truth about Virgil, send him to jail."

"And Tammy along with him." She turned away, the weight of the situation settled firmly on her shoulders. The Christmas lights blurred with the sudden tears crowding her eyes.

He came near and wrapped her in an embrace, his chin resting on the top of her head. "It's gonna be okay. We'll find a way out of this."

His arms were both solid and gentle, the beat of his heart steadying against her ear. "I'm not good at sneaking around, hiding the truth. I feel…"

"Tense as a cat in a rocking chair factory?"

She smiled, looking up into the denim wash of his eyes. "Yeah, something like that. A cook I used to work with used that one, too."

"We're going to unravel all this, but in the meantime, let me get you settled in the saddlery, okay?"

She nodded, casting a longing glance down the hallway into the kitchen.

"You want to go cook somethin', don't you?"

"Yeah. That's when everything makes sense to me, when I'm cooking for people."

"All right, then," he said, taking her hand and leading her to the kitchen. "Let's see what we can do about that."

She was tentative at first, in someone else's kitchen, but soon he saw her shoulders relax and the tension drain from her expression as she stirred up a creamy batter and turned out a perfect circle into a sizzling frying pan. The batter transformed into a crisped brown pancake. Her slender hands moved around the stove as easily as his held the reins. He could watch her cook all day, he realized.

"This is ridiculous," she said. "You just ate."

"My philosophy is that life's uncertain and there's always room for more."

Laughing, she slid the pancake onto a plate.

The fragrance of it took him back to his childhood kitchen, his mom frying up funny-faced pancakes for him and Helen. He hadn't thought of those silly things in years. He blinked away the memory and ate the pancake with gusto.

"Delicious," he said.

"You'd say that anyway."

"Nah. Light and fluffy. Who taught you how to cook? No offense to your sister, but she isn't exactly the Betty Crocker type. Between the two of us, we couldn't even make a sandwich." He wasn't sure he should have made reference to him and Tammy together, but being with Maggie loosened his tongue. She was so very different from her twin.

"This reminds me of cooking in our restaurant one Christmastime. Two cooks came down with the flu and all of the waitresses were stuck on the freeway after a pileup. Tammy and I were only sixteen, but I manned the kitchen along with our lone cook, and she waitressed her heart out next to Mom and Aunt Linda." She laughed. "I don't think the patrons were totally wowed with the food I put out, but Daddy was impressed enough with my work ethic to let me take an afterschool shift as a sous chef. He said we should start my cooking education at the beginning, so we spent a whole day just on breakfast foods. Pancakes were the first thing

Daddy taught me how to cook, but Tammy never wanted to learn. I was so proud of myself."

A pang cut somewhere inside him. "It's a good thing, to love your daddy."

"I do. I adore him. He and mom owned a restaurant for decades until a fire burned it down fifteen years ago. Daddy was out getting supplies when it happened. I was manning the kitchen with a couple of other employees when the grease caught and set fire to the ventilation hood. It spread from there. All the employees got out but…" She became suddenly busy cleaning the counter.

"But?" he prompted.

"I tried to put out the fire, stupidly, instead of leaving like a smart person would have. For a while it seemed like I'd actually managed to snuff it out, but I passed out due to smoke inhalation. I would have died if Tammy hadn't dragged me out. We were seventeen. She saved my life."

He could imagine Tammy doing something like that and, what's more, he found it easy to believe that Maggie would be the type to risk everything to save what her father loved. "She did the world a favor."

Maggie's cheeks went rosy. She continued wiping the already clean counter. "Anyway, that's my mission in life, to buy a place and re-open Daddy's restaurant. He's not working now, staying home to take care of Mom since she got breast cancer, but he still cooks every day. I'm going to call it Ruby's like he did. That's my mom's name." She shot him a shy smile. "We'll serve plenty of pancakes, no doubt."

Liam wanted her to go on talking, so he could listen to the quiet passion in her words, watch the glimmer of love and pride twined in the syllables. The cadence of her voice was as soothing as an easy ride across brilliant acres of ranch land. He willed her to continue. Instead she asked him a question as she washed the pan and spatula. "What about your family? You said your mom died. Is your father still living?"

"Yeah, lives somewhere in Colorado, last I heard."

Her lips curved in a tender expression that made his throat thicken.

"You're not close, I take it?"

The words were so soft he could not bear it another moment. "Aw, you don't want to hear about my old man and me," he said, twirling the fork in his fingers. "It's a sad tale that comes out sounding like a country-and-western song."

She didn't take the bait, her gaze intensifying. "It's your turn to share," she said gently.

He shrugged and cleared his throat. Was this

the price to be paid for listening to someone share her heart? It was a price he'd never been eager to pay before with another woman. Listening and supporting, sure, but sharing his own stuff? He'd never told anyone on the ranch, not even Tammy, the truth about his father. Squashing down the discomfort, he made his mouth say the words. "Dad couldn't be a dad after Mom died. That's about all there is to it."

She wanted more and he wanted to give it to her, but how could he say it? How could he tell her how his dad had abdicated his role? Explain how Liam had become a professional charmer, fooling everyone into thinking they had a functional parent when Liam was basically running the household at age seven? He forced a yawn. "Man, it's getting late. Let's get you settled in for the night."

He felt her gaze linger on his back as he turned away. *Share with her*, his heart commanded. But the words could not find their way through the layers he'd grown, new identities he'd assumed, uniforms he'd put on, masks he'd made. No one could get through all those layers. Tammy hadn't; he hadn't wanted her to. He wasn't sure he even knew himself how to unwrap all the trappings and lay bare his soul.

He felt Maggie draw next to him and then her arm was around his shoulders and he was turning, lost in those eyes the color of the forest in autumn. Though he knew he shouldn't, he allowed his palms to trace the contours of her shoulders.

"If it helps, my father always told us he was a poor excuse for our real Father, but he was doing the best he could," she said.

He held back a derisive snort. "That's not my story. My old man didn't do his best, not even close. He gave up when it got too hard, instead of getting help."

"I'm sorry," she said and there was such sincerity in her voice, such tenderness.

He shrugged, trying to sound cavalier. "Doesn't matter. I became pretty good at being a man and taking care of Helen. We didn't need him. Don't need him now. I can take care of everything."

Then suddenly the reality hit him again. He was being gradually unmanned one day at a time, stripped of his hearing. "Until I'm stone-deaf anyway." Had he said that aloud? Almost admitted that deepest fear? Or had he infused it with the right amount of cocky humor? His heart hammered in his chest as her gaze captured his.

She didn't say a word, just embraced him, her cheek on his chest. What was she thinking? Sorry that she'd asked? Thinking him foolish?

Worst of all, pitying him for his disability and his tattered past? But as the embrace warmed him, his senses thrilled at the feel of her. With the sweetness of maple syrup still on his tongue, he found he did not care so much.

The moment passed. They made their way, her to the saddlery and him to the bunkhouse, yet the strange sensation of calm lasted well through the night. Thinking of her nestled safe, cocooned at the ranch he loved, he let himself drift off to sleep.

TEN

Maggie awoke in the saddlery, momentarily disoriented. She inhaled deeply the fragrance of leather. As she dressed, she considered what had passed between her and Liam the night before.

Tammy had said Liam was fun to be with, highly intelligent with a ferocious wit, but he wasn't the one for her. She wondered if Liam had ever told Tammy about his father and why he had chosen to share the precious burden with her. And why was she pondering her relationship with Liam in the first place? Deep down he was much more than the happy-go-lucky cowboy he tried so hard to portray, but that was not her business. He was only helping her because of his history with Tammy and she would be wise to remember that pertinent fact. *You're Tammy's sister to him and that's all.* Still, she could not quite let go of the feel of his arms around her.

Resolved to move ahead, and grateful that the

Chuckwagon was closed on parade day, she let herself out of the tiny living space to find Liam in the workshop area holding two mugs of coffee. Jingles trotted over to greet her. She accepted the coffee and the dog licks with a laugh.

"Do you go everywhere with this dog?"

He rolled his eyes. "I can't get rid of him. He's like a shadow."

She drank the coffee, unable to sustain her good cheer against a sudden wave of tension. "I'm dreading this morning. I don't want to say the wrong thing and get my sister in more trouble. I called her earlier and told her about the police and Joe."

"How'd she take it?"

"She cried and said she'd text him and meet us at the station. I told her I could handle it alone, but she won't hear of it."

"A stubborn Lofton sister? Imagine that."

"No more stubborn than a Pike sibling," Maggie said.

"Fair point."

"I'm just not suited for this kind of thing. My sister's always been the one to seek out drama and danger. She's exotic gourmet food and I'm more of a meat loaf and mashed potatoes temperament. Plain Jane."

"Being good at what you love doesn't make you plain."

She shrugged. "I'm not the kind of woman most men seek out, let's just say."

"Only the smart men."

She quirked a look at him. "Most men prefer my sister's type, and I don't blame them. You, for example."

Liam gulped his coffee a little too fast. "Tam is a wonderful woman, but don't sell yourself short because you're different." He smiled around his mug. "I think I'm beginning to recognize I like meat loaf and mashed potatoes more than exotic food." His blue gaze lingered on her a moment and then he got busy looking out the window and checking the time on his phone as if he was trying to distract himself and her from what he'd just said.

She was not quite sure how to respond. It felt both strange and soothing to be able to mention his relationship with Tammy, but she was not sure how to continue, or if she wanted to. Tammy's ex was becoming a fixture in her soul whether she wanted to recognize it or not, but she could not assume he felt the same way, regardless of their kitchen chitchat.

They finished their coffee, the conversation light and practical as they got in Liam's truck and delivered the muffins they'd taken from the van to the Veteran's Hall. They rode to the police station, past streets that were being barricaded.

"Does everyone in town turn out for the parade?"

"Yes, ma'am."

She heard Jingles snuffling around a box in the back seat.

"Stay outta there," he commanded. "That's for the parade."

"Are you helping?"

He grinned. "Oh yeah. Wouldn't miss it. Not to brag, but really, I'm kinda a star with the under ten crowd. Kicks off in about an hour." He shot her a look from under the brim of his cowboy hat. "You, uh, want to go? I mean, it's the main holiday attraction around here aside from the Train of Lights. Tammy went with me last year and…" Liam did not exactly blush, but the conversation sputtered and died.

"It's okay," she said. "We both know you dated my sister. It doesn't need to be a taboo topic."

"It's just…weird."

"Yes, weird."

"I mean, you're not weird. I was just, er, saying the situation was out of the ordinary, in a good way but…"

The giggles started, probably borne both of her growing nervousness about the police meeting and the humor of seeing the self-assured cowboy pink with embarrassment.

He sighed, gaze riveted on the road ahead. "I

think I'd better put myself on a talking time-out before any more stupidity materializes."

"It's okay, really," she said when the giggles subsided. "No need for that. Besides, it's very entertaining watching you all off-kilter."

"Great. Glad I can provide some amusement."

"It's out of the ordinary for me, too." She squared her shoulders. "We've had a rule in the past...sisters' exes are strictly off-limits." *But Tammy always said rules were made to be broken.* She was glad she kept that last bit to herself.

He nodded. "Of course. Sure. Absolutely. Anyway, uh, here we are." The police station was a modest one-story building. A receptionist greeted them and pointed them to Danny Patron's office.

The chief of police was a red-haired man in his early forties with a forthcoming smile and a photo of three young daughters on his desk. Several crayoned pictures festooned the corner bulletin board and a selection of plastic action figures was arranged in a row around his computer.

He rose when they came in and gestured for Maggie to take a chair. Tammy entered next, holding on to Helen's arm and limping. Maggie hugged her sister fiercely and drew her into the next chair. Liam offered his seat to Helen, but she refused.

"I have to pop across the street to make sure my Lodge guests have their reserved seating area for the parade. See you in a few."

Danny grinned as he looked from Tammy to Maggie. "Because I am a keen police observer, I'm going to speculate you two are fraternal twins."

Maggie smiled. "Yes, sir."

"No need for 'sir.' You can call me Danny—" he winked "—or Head Bottle Washer, whichever you prefer. Can I get you some terrible coffee? It's the only kind we serve, but it's hot."

Both sisters laughed, declined the offer, and Maggie felt a twinge of hope. Maybe this would work out all right coming clean with the police. She launched into the story with Tammy adding notes as she went.

"I think I get the gist of it from your perspective," Danny said.

"It's the truth," Tammy insisted. "I would never steal from Bill. I just wanted to protect the jewelry until I could get to the police. It was an impulsive decision." She sighed. "I'm sort of famous for those."

Maggie squeezed her hand, concerned about her sister's pallor. "Impulsive, not criminal."

"Not in the eyes of the law," Tammy said, her voice wobbling.

Danny jotted something on the notepad in front of him, his smile disappearing. "And I'll talk to the Sand Dune police and your boyfriend Joe to corroborate, but there's something you should know. Come with me."

Maggie helped her sister follow Danny and Liam down the hall into a conference room. Two people were already seated there, an elderly man and Virgil Salvador.

Panic slashed through Maggie at the sight of him. Virgil was composed, legs crossed, dressed in nice slacks and a button-up shirt.

"They arrived ahead of you," Danny said, "and they've got a different story to tell."

Virgil looked from Maggie to Tammy, his eyes roving in a way that made Maggie go cold inside. "I never knew you had a sister, Tammy." He smiled. "She's beautiful, too. Is she a thief like you?"

Liam wanted to knock the smug smile clean off Virgil's mug, but Maggie commanded Danny's attention. "I don't know what he's told you, but he almost killed me at the lighthouse on Wednesday night."

Danny frowned. "And you're just reporting this?"

Maggie's cheeks went rosy. "Liam urged me to, but I was waiting to contact my sister. That was foolish, I see that now."

Liam gave her an encouraging nod. "She was under pressure and scared for her sister."

"Okay. Timing aside, can you make a positive ID?" Danny said. "Did you see his face?"

"No," Maggie admitted. "I was blinded by the lighthouse beacon."

"Liam?" Danny rubbed his nose. "You were there. Can you ID Virgil as the lighthouse attacker?"

Liam grunted. "Same height and build, and I know his voice. That's him, but no, I didn't see his face clearly."

Virgil's smile broadened. "You see? I told you Tammy would make up any story to get herself out of trouble. Doesn't surprise me that she's got her sister helping."

Liam stood taller. There was no way he was going to let the women be railroaded by some gel-haired slicker in loafers. "The trailer. Virgil met Maggie there for sure. Threatened her."

"I was merely offering to help as someone trashed her trailer."

"You did it," Liam said.

"Can you prove it?" Virgil said.

He ground his teeth. Knowing and proving

were two different things as Mitch had pointed out to him on occasion.

"Didn't think so," Virgil said. "The fact of the matter is that Tammy stole my uncle's jewelry. That hurt us both deeply, because we are really fond of her. We never imagined she could do anything like that."

Tammy took a step toward Bill. "I didn't... I mean... I was trying to help keep your wife's things safe. Please, Bill. I can't stand having you think I would steal from you."

Bill looked from face to face, his expression dazed. He did not answer Tammy. Virgil patted his shoulder. "My uncle is confused from time to time. It's been so hard since his wife passed away. She fell down the stairs, so it was very unexpected. He has had a difficult time adjusting. He hardly slept at all last night."

"Are you Mr. Salvador's heir, Virgil? Or his legal guardian?" Danny's expression was still pleasant, but the question caught Virgil by surprise.

Liam smiled inwardly. *Go get 'em, Head Bottle Washer.*

Virgil straightened in his chair. "No. His granddaughter, Vivian Salvador, is heir to the property. She's living in France, managing three children by herself, since her husband left her. I moved in about six months ago at Bill's request, since she's too busy with her own life to help him." A tiny flicker of disappointment with just a smear of compassion colored his tone. Liam smothered a snort. The guy changed emotions to suit his purpose like a chameleon. "That's why we hired Tammy. Bill needed a live-in aide." Virgil sighed. "I just never thought it would come to this."

Tammy knelt next to Bill's chair, her eyes pleading.

Bill seemed to recognize her and he put a wrinkled hand atop hers. "There you are, Tammy. Don't look so sad." A smile wreathed his face in creases. "I've missed you."

"I've missed you, too." Tammy struggled to hold her tears back. "Your hands are cold."

Liam took off his jacket and laid it over Bill's shoulders, earning a hostile glare from Virgil. Didn't matter a whit to Liam. You didn't let an elderly man sit there feeling cold.

He flashed back to his own grandfather, who'd been ailing long before his mother's accident. At his daughter's funeral, as Liam's mother was laid into the ground, Grandpa Lou had sprinkled rose petals atop the grave. Liam remembered how his hand had shaken like Bill's, the shoulders stooped with grief and age. Was there any pain worse than burying your child? Or your wife? Liam stepped back and away from the unexpected memory. He hadn't spent much time putting himself in his father's shoes, emotionally anyway.

"Will you go home with us?" Bill gripped Tammy's fingers. "I want to go back to the house. I... I don't like it here."

He saw rather than heard Tammy gulp back a sob. "I'm sorry, Bill. I can't right now."

Virgil stood, clasping Bill's shoulder and staring Tammy down. "We don't want this to get ugly. Tell the truth and stop trying to cover yourself by insinuating I was arranging to have the jewelry stolen. I have never even touched those jewels."

"You were on the phone, giving someone the all clear to steal them," Tammy snapped.

Danny raised a palm. "First things first. Where is the jewelry now, Tammy?"

Maggie held Tammy's arm for support. "I don't remember where I left it. I had a head injury in the accident Virgil caused."

"It was a hit-and-run, as the Sand Dune Police will tell you," Virgil said to Danny before he cocked his chin at Tammy, his expression ripe with what looked to be compassion. "You can come up with a better story than that. I understand people make mistakes. I do. I've made my share of them, believe me. If you've already fenced the jewelry, there's no need to go any further with this. Tell me, and stop accusing me, and this all goes away."

"That would be grand for you, wouldn't it?" Liam interjected. "Tammy admits she stole the jewelry and takes the punishment so you can finish up your little insurance fraud game?" Liam's fierce glare was aimed directly at Virgil. "Take the settlement for yourself?"

Virgil's smile tightened into something less pleasant. "She's a convincing liar. I see she's persuaded you, too." His eyes narrowed. "You're her ex-boyfriend, right? Maybe she's looking to get back together with you. She's a pretty girl, free-spirited, so you'd probably like nothing better, huh?" His eyes shifted to Maggie. "Or have you moved on to the sister?"

Liam closed the gap between them. If it wasn't for the frightened elderly man between them, he'd have closed it further.

Danny held up a warning palm. "Easy, gentlemen. Let's keep it civil."

Heat coursed through Liam's veins. "You're not going to make it look like either one of these women is the bad guy here, Virgil."

"I don't have to." He pulled his phone from his pocket. "This will tell you everything you need to know." With a tap of his finger, a video played. There was no sound. The picture showed Tammy running from the house with a black box under her arm. "If you'd like," Virgil said, "I can show you the rest. It's clearly Tammy hopping into her green Corvette and speeding away down the street."

He waggled the phone. "You see? You can't really argue with video proof, can you? Tammy stole the jewelry. I had nothing to do with it."

Tammy began to shiver. Maggie clasped her shoulders, saying, "We already told you why she did that. Surely that counts for something. She was on her way to see you, Chief. She would have explained it then, but you weren't in and she panicked. Please."

Liam hated the pleading tone in Maggie's words. "Danny, can't you help us out here?" he said through gritted teeth.

Danny considered the group, the room so still it seemed as though they were all frozen in some sort of bizarre tableau. Then he shook his head and turned to Tammy. "I'm sorry, Miss Lofton, but if Mr. Salvador wishes to press charges, I'm afraid I'll have to arrest you."

ELEVEN

Maggie's stomach fisted into a tight knot as her greatest fear began to unfold before her. This could not be happening.

"No," she said, struggling to keep her tone steady. "My sister was trying to protect Bill, not hurt him."

Virgil shrugged. "As I said, video doesn't lie. She's a thief."

A voice exploded from the doorway. "No way. Tammy is not guilty of any wrongdoing and you know it full well." Joe stood, hands on hips, glowering at Virgil.

Maggie saw Liam startle. He had not heard Joe approach.

Tammy cried out and hobbled over to him. He wrapped her in a tight embrace. "It's okay, baby. I'm here now."

"Who are you, sir?" Danny asked.

"Joe Albertson. I'm Tammy's boyfriend. I did some computer programming work for Bill Salvador and that's how I met Tammy." He shot a look at Virgil. "You and I both know Tammy would never steal from Bill. It doesn't matter what your video says."

Virgil's expression clouded and he was quiet for a long moment. When he spoke, his voice was cold. "I am not as inclined to fall for her story as her boyfriend—" he shot a look at Liam "—or her ex-boyfriend."

Joe was whispering into Tammy's ear, kissing her temples and smoothing her hair.

Maggie could not help glancing at Liam. He appeared more contemplative than upset at Joe's attention to Tammy. For some reason, it comforted her. She found Liam had reached for her hand and she clutched it for all she was worth. This could not be happening. Her sister could not be going to jail.

Virgil stared at Joe and Tammy, a wash of some emotion she could not identify twisting his features. "Uncle Bill is tired right now. We'll have to go home and talk it over about pressing charges. Then we'll decide whether or not Tammy is going to jail."

Danny picked up his buzzing cell phone and stepped out as he launched into a conversation.

Virgil took his uncle's forearm, letting Liam's jacket fall to the floor before he led him to the door, stopping next to Maggie. "All she has to do is admit she was lying about me, and we'll ask the judge for lenience," he said, low and hard. "Otherwise I've got a pawnbroker who will swear she has stolen other things from Bill and pawned them. It'll be a much longer sentence." He was level with Maggie when he added in a voice no louder than a whisper, "No more excuses. Give me what I want or I'll hurt you both."

Liam took an angry step forward. "What did you say?"

Virgil smiled. "Ask your new girlfriend."

Virgil and Bill passed through and out of the conference room.

Maggie exhaled and bent over, trying to stem the sudden dizziness she felt. *I'll hurt you both.*

Danny darted a look at Maggie as he entered the room. "What did I miss?"

She strove for calm. "He said he'd hurt us if I don't cooperate—not loudly enough for anyone else to hear, of course."

Liam's arm was strong and steady around her. "Coward. We'll check him out. Get something we can use. He won't touch either one of you."

The radio on Danny's hip buzzed with static. "Like Liam says, it gives us time to investigate, talk to this pawnbroker, look at Virgil's history."

"Then you believe me?" Tammy said through tears.

He grinned. "I didn't get to be the Head Bottle Washer by not sniffing out the truth." He held up a hand. "That said, I have to act on the evidence and, right now, that all points to you, Miss Lofton."

She bit her lip and Joe kissed her hair. "Don't worry. We'll find a way."

Danny clicked off his radio. "I have to go help with the parade details, but I'm just saying that the pressure's on Virgil now, too. An insurance investigator called earlier, asking to meet with me. Virgil knows he's being looked at through a microscope. They aren't going to pay out until they're thoroughly satisfied they're not being defrauded."

Maggie's mind began to churn through possible angles.

Danny continued. "I'm going to handle this like a regular investigation until charges are brought. I have to be impartial, no matter who's involved or what my personal feelings are."

"Fair enough," Liam said. "You do what you need to and we'll do the same."

"All aboveboard and nice and legal?"

"Yes, sir."

Maggie went to Tammy and handed her some tissues while Joe patted her back.

"Gonna be okay, Tammy. You'll see," he said.

Maggie turned in time to hear Danny speak in lowered tones to Liam.

"You got this, cowboy?"

"What do you mean?"

"One ex-girlfriend and one sister equals a whole lot of trouble on my adding machine tape."

Liam lifted a shoulder. "Exes' sisters are strictly off-limits."

Exes' sisters. That's what she was to Liam, nothing more.

Maggie's breath hitched and she busied herself fetching more tissues that her sister did not need. Why should it bother her? She wasn't in the market for a boyfriend anyway, especially not Liam.

You blew into town pretending to be Tammy, remember? He'd stuck his neck out because of his history with her sister and because he was a good man, a man of honor.

How could she know that after only a few days in his company? But she did know it from the tiniest clues: his tenderness with Charlie, the sharing of his jacket with a confused old man.

Then why did she feel something deeper than gratitude and admiration? As if they'd shared something more in those moments in the kitchen over pancakes.

Strictly off-limits, her memory repeated.

It was best for her to remember that.

* * *

Helen joined them outside. Jingles set up a racket as soon as he saw Liam, so Liam let him loose from the truck. They introduced Joe to Helen and Jingles.

"I want to stay close to Tammy at the Lodge," Joe announced.

Helen shook her head, stalling Liam's disapproving comment. "I'm sorry, but the Lodge is full and she's staying in my bedroom."

"I'll sleep in a storage room or on the floor, anything."

"If you think you're sleeping in my sister's room," Liam snapped, louder than he'd meant, "you've got another thing coming."

Apparently his tone penetrated Joe's bubbling emotions. He breathed out and shoved the glasses up farther on his nose, a flush creeping across his pale cheeks. "No, no, of course not. I'm sorry. I guess I'm a little wired after those threats. I'll find a place in town and help all I can. We've gotta find the jewelry."

Tammy winced. "He might just decide to kill us anyway."

Liam considered that. "Virgil wants to get his hands on the jewelry bad, because if it's recovered, his insurance scam goes up in flames. Or maybe he wants to double-dip to both fence the necklace and collect the insurance. He's desperate."

"How desperate?" Helen asked.

Joe pursed his lips. "When I was working in Bill's house, I saw Virgil reading a couple of letters that looked like past due notices. He might be in some deep financial trouble."

Did that make him desperate enough to harm Tammy or Maggie even after the police were involved? Brazen enough to lie flat-out to a cop and manipulate an old man? Yeah. Liam figured there weren't too many more lines Virgil wouldn't cross. He'd demonstrated as much. He wasn't afraid to threaten, hurt and probably kill.

Helen straightened her hat against the winter breeze. "So the only way to derail Virgil's plans is to find the jewelry before the insurance pays out and somehow prove Virgil's a crook."

A smile wreathed Liam's face. "Well, there's nothing I like better than a challenge."

"Do you really think we can do this?" Maggie asked.

He laughed, laying on his thickest country twang. "Does a raccoon wear a mask?"

"I guess the answer's yes, then?" Maggie said with a giggle.

"I reckon so," Liam said.

Helen shook her head. "My brother the hayseed who got a perfect score on his SATs the first time he took them. Don't let him fool you. He loves it when people underestimate him."

She turned to Tammy. "Let's get you back to bed. You look all-in."

Joe kissed her goodbye. "I'm going to get you a new phone. I'll drop it by the Lodge later, okay?" He walked with them, his arm around her protectively.

"He seems to really love her," Maggie said wistfully.

"Maybe," Liam said. "Jury's still out. But he's growing on me."

"Me, too. I like the way he stood up to Virgil."

"Not bad for a computer programmer." Liam frowned and went quiet.

She crinkled her nose at him. "Why do you look so thoughtful all of a sudden?"

"I'm thinking about the mission."

"The mission?"

"Uh-huh. On a mission you got to know a few things—what you need to accomplish, how to get there and what success will look like." He exhaled. "We know all that now."

"We do?"

He ticked it off on his fingers. "Going to get the jewelry back to mess up Virgil's plans, send him to jail, and keep him from getting near you and Tammy. Simple."

"It doesn't seem simple to me."

"Stick with me, Miss Lofton. I'm locked, loaded and ready."

She pointed to a Santa hat sticking out of his back pocket. "Does that include your horse or your sleigh?"

He took off his cowboy hat and clapped on the red one, complete with white fur trim. Jingles perked up. "I'm ready to get this parade started and deliver up some holiday cheer so we can get back to stalking our prey." He slid a candy cane from his pocket.

She laughed. "Did they teach you that in the Green Berets, too?"

"Believe it or not, we did a lot of candy diplomacy when I was in Kunar Province, like Mitch said. Sometimes it was literally handing sweets to the kids, or maybe mediating disputes between elders, or training indigenous troops. Whatever it took to be a force multiplier." He held out a crooked arm. "So what do you say, Maggie? Ready to join up for parade duty?" He paused. "I want you close in case Virgil is sticking around town, waiting for another chance."

Maggie shivered and looked down the street toward the Chuckwagon.

He followed her gaze. "Hungry?" Liam said. "We can grab something at the Lodge after the parade."

"No, not hungry. I was thinking I owe Nan and Tiny an apology for deceiving them. I didn't flat-out tell them I was Tammy, but I let them think it."

"You had good reasons."

She shrugged. "It was still a deceit. I need to apologize now that we've told the police everything. I'm going to pop in since I know they're prepping for the dinner hour, and then I'll meet you at parade central."

"Not wild about that idea."

"I've got my phone and plenty of company."

"All right, but I'd like you to watch the parade with Mitch and Charlie. Safety in numbers."

"Okay. Ten minutes at the Chuckwagon, then you can point me to Mitch and Charlie."

He angled a look at her. "Okay. I'll text Mitch and find out where he is exactly. Crowds are only going to get worse from here, so we need to get plans in place."

"Yes, sir."

"No need for official titles. Call me Cowboy Santa."

She laughed, tipping her face to the sky, and the sunlight coaxed sparkles in her hair. His pulse stirred.

Strictly off-limits, he reminded himself as she headed to the Chuckwagon.

TWELVE

A half hour later, feeling relieved to have offered her humble apology, Maggie joined in the melee behind the post office, the starting point for the parade. The lot was jammed with participants, floats, classic cars and uniformed Scout troops. She found Liam and Chad next to a trailer.

Liam stroked the sleek sides of his black horse, whose harness sparkled with tinsel. She spied a saddlebag filled with candy canes.

Chad quietly brushed down his brown mare, similarly decorated. He gave her a silent head bob.

"How'd it go with Nan?" Liam asked her.

"She graciously forgave me and she wants me to stay on when this whole mess is resolved."

"Who wouldn't? I mean…" He patted Streak. "Tiny says you cook like a master and I know for a fact your pancakes are top-shelf."

She was pleased at his praise. Too pleased, she scolded herself. "All set for the parade?"

He nodded and grimaced. "Yeah, but I got me a problem," Liam looked down at Jingles, who was sporting a set of light-up antlers. "Watch."

He tossed a candy cane from the saddlebag and Jingles promptly snatched it from midair, grinning around the edges of the candy. "Drop it," he thundered and Jingles obeyed, tail wagging. "See what I mean? How am I s'posed to throw candy to the kids with this dog snatching it all up? Gonna have to lock him in the truck, but he'll howl something fierce the whole time."

She held her amusement in check. "Why don't you let him keep one?"

A frown creased his forehead. "What?"

She moved closer, spoke louder. "He wants one for himself, I think."

"I never thought of that." He unwrapped a cane, tossed it, and Jingles snatched it up. "All right, then. You can have that one, but no more," he said to the dog. Warily he tossed another. Jingles remained where he was, tail wagging, content with the one already in his mouth.

The look of wonder Liam gave her under that Santa hat was purely irresistible.

"That was nothing short of amazing," he said. "You are incredible."

His admiration made her look away, twirling

the edges of the Christmas scarf Aunt Ginny had insisted she wear. "So where should I find Mitch?"

"Three blocks down on the left. I'll double back and meet you there after the parade."

"All right. I'll be on the lookout to catch a candy cane."

He saluted and she made her way along the crowded sidewalk.

She craned her neck every which way but could not see Mitch through all the bystanders. The crowd swelled and jostled until she found herself nestled into a spot against one of the Chuckwagon's massive metal wheels. The throng spread out in front of her; little families with red-cheeked children, older folks in camping chairs. Practically the entire town had assembled, along with a hefty dose of visitors mixed in from what she could discern. All around there was holiday cheer and merriment, and she would have given anything to enjoy it with her sister, free from the worry of Virgil. In spite of her distress, she found herself humming along to the approaching marching band's Christmas carol medley. Their white uniforms and feather plumes flashed in the sunshine. She was caught up in the excitement until she heard a name.

"Yoriko."

She jerked a look to her right. Two women were saying goodbye, talking loudly to be heard over the clamor of the marching band. The younger woman left, leaving a lady with a dark fringe of bangs, wearing a green jacket, smiling at the parade.

Maggie dodged in and around spectators and hastened over. "Hello, Yoriko?" She took in the woman's surprise. "I'm Maggie Lofton. You know my sister Tammy."

The woman gave a small nod before she smiled. "Yes. For a moment, I thought that's who you were."

"Twins," Maggie explained. She was jostled from behind; a figure bundled in a down vest, wearing a ski cap. He did not turn and Maggie felt a strange ripple of dread wash over her, but the figure moved away. The whole situation was making her paranoid. She refocused on Yoriko. "You and my sister are friends?"

"Yes. I am a glassblower and she did some work painting ornaments for me at my shop."

"Have you seen her recently?"

Yoriko nodded and Maggie's spirits leaped.

"Wednesday."

The band was almost adjacent now, the beat of the drums vibrating in Maggie's chest. She pressed closer. "This is going to sound strange, but Tammy is having trouble remembering things due to a head injury. Did she, by chance, leave something at your place?"

The crash of music grew almost deafening. Maggie could not hear the reply, but her pulse zinged at the woman's nod. Her mouth moved, the words swallowed up in the clamor.

"I'm sorry," Maggie called out. "I can't hear you."

Yoriko pulled a business card from her coat pocket. "Come see me," she said. "Monday afternoon. I have an event tomorrow and I won't be home until then."

The band's performance was met with thunderous applause and the crowd swelled as bystanders stood to get a better look. Liam was approaching, tall and easy on his horse, scattering candy canes to the children in the crowd. Jingles followed dutifully along, his own candy prize clutched between his teeth. Chad worked the other side of the street. Maggie noted how his rare smile transformed his whole demeanor. Such a quiet man, yet kind and straightforward, like the rest of the Roughwater Ranch clan.

Maggie caught sight of a little boy high up on a pair of sturdy shoulders. Charlie, waving wildly to his uncle Liam. Finally she'd found Mitch and his son, but there was no way to get to them. Liam stopped in front of Charlie and prompted his horse. Streak executed a simple bow on one knee, which thrilled both Charlie and the crowd. Then Liam tossed Charlie a candy cane. Mitch caught it and handed it to the excited boy. Maggie's heart melted at the exchange between Liam and his nephew.

As Chad and Liam drew closer, eager youngsters pushed to the front to retrieve the sweets and Maggie was elbowed to the back. When she looked around for Yoriko, she had disappeared into the milling spectators.

Maggie was up against the wagon wheel when the man with the down vest stepped in front of her, blocking her way. Fear kicked wild in her gut.

"Good parade," Virgil said.

"Stay away from me," she said, scanning for the nearest stranger.

"Oh, I'm just taking in the sights. Uncle Bill was tired, so I left him to nap in the car. Couldn't miss the Driftwood Christmas Parade."

Maggie desperately tried to catch Liam's attention, but there were dozens of wriggling kids and standing parents trying to wrangle them. The scent of Virgil's cologne sickened her. *Stay calm*, she commanded herself. *He wants the jewelry. You can leverage that.*

"I've been doing a bit of thinking." He stepped closer, one hand in his pocket. Concealing a knife? He could hurt her and no one would even hear her scream over the roar of the crowd. The wagon wheel boxed her in to her right. She eased to her left in preparation to run.

Virgil went on, perfectly at ease. "If Tammy told you where those jewels are, maybe you're planning on retrieving them. Maybe you're hoping to keep them for yourself?"

"You are delusional. If you come nearer, I will scream."

A stagecoach pulling Santa was coming into view and the crowd went wild with cheers.

"But who would hear you?" Virgil said.

She swallowed down her fear and forced her chin up. "Let's find out."

"Enough. You give me the jewelry and I make the video go away. The insurance company doesn't require visual proof of a theft. I'll say I never ID'd the thief. They pay out. Tammy stays out of jail. Bill gets his jewelry back. Everybody wins. If you don't do what I want…" He paused. "Then I am going to kill you and your sister. Is that clear enough for you?"

Maggie almost choked on her fear. "You're going to jail," she managed to force out.

"For what? There's no one to overhear this conversation and I promise no one will be able to prove I murdered you two. I'm clever, you see."

She tried frantically to still her wildly beating

heart. "We'll tell your uncle about how you're manipulating him. That's elder abuse."

Hatred tightened his mouth. "He's not poor, and he's lorded it over my family for generations. His wife was just like him. He doesn't deserve what he has and neither did his old harpie of a wife. I'm glad she died in that fall."

His outburst shocked her into silence for a moment. She wondered for a fleeting moment if Virgil had had something to do with Bill's wife's accident. The shock gave way to anger, thinking about the sweet man who'd held Tammy's hands, asking her to stay. She forced herself to stand straight. "Oh, I'm going to give the jewelry to the police, Virgil, and you won't get that payout. You're going to jail."

His nostrils flared. "Pretending to be Tammy, that was a good trick, but I saw through that ruse. I'm smart and I'm determined."

"Ditto," she said, edging farther away.

His grimace changed to a wide smile. "You're so beautiful when you're passionate about something, almost as beautiful as your sister," he said, "and sassy. Those are the same things I love about Tammy."

Maggie recoiled, dumb with disgust.

He looked wistful. "We would have been so

good together, the perfect couple." He laughed. "Christmas card material."

"My sister would never be with someone like you, a greedy liar."

His smile vanished. "Are you so sure of that? Maybe your sister isn't as smart as you think. Maybe you both aren't. You'll both be easy to kill. You won't even see it coming."

She prepared herself for a fast lunge, a hard shove to his shoulder, her one shot at an escape.

"Be careful, Maggie. You don't want to be standing between a man and his goals. Accidents happen."

"You don't have the power to threaten me," Maggie forced out, wishing she felt the truth of the words.

He touched the end of her scarf, softly at first and then clenching with such hard force that his fingernails stabbed through the gauzy fabric. In a flash he'd pulled it tight. Her hands flew to her throat as he began to strangle her.

"Not a threat. A promise," he whispered.

A scream rose in her throat, caught in her closing windpipe. She batted at his fists, her body screaming for air.

"Don't forget our little conversation," he murmured into her ear. He shoved her away and her back slammed into the wagon wheel, the cold steel biting into her skin from behind as she coughed and gasped.

Liam finally caught sight of Maggie. There was a man blocking his view, body turned from the parade. Facing away from the parade? Suspicion turned to alarm. "Chad," he yelled.

Chad whipped a look at him. There was no time to explain and Chad wouldn't require any more information anyway. Liam needed help, that was all Chad had to know. Chad immediately began to part the crowd, herding the people away from the Chuckwagon like he did with cattle when they separated them to be tagged. As a space cleared, Liam urged Streak forward, calling for the remaining people to move aside. They did so, their attention on Santa and the stagecoach approaching to Liam's rear. He got clear just as Maggie darted past the Chuckwagon, running toward the barricade at the end of the street.

He flicked Streak into a trot and caught up with her.

"Maggie," he called.

She jerked a look over her shoulder, stumbling to a stop. Acting on instinct, he reached down and swung her up in front of him, riding them away from the hubbub. Her body shook within the circle of his arms as he slowed the horse to a stop.

"I've got you," he murmured into her hair. She couldn't do much more than try to catch her breath and he let her, crooning comfort and holding her close. He scanned the crowd for the guy he'd seen, with no sign of him.

She stammered through a story about Virgil that made Liam wheel Streak around, searching for him. "Gone. We'll tell the cops and find him."

"There were no witnesses, again."

"I don't care. He's not gonna get away with hurting you."

Chad rode up.

"Virgil got close," Liam said. "He tried to choke her. He's melted away into the crowd. Keep your eyes out for him."

Chad nodded. "I'll call Mitch," he said before leading the horse away.

"I'll do the same with Danny." By the time he finished leaving a message, Maggie was calmer. He dismounted and helped her down.

She was still shivering, so he wrapped her up close, warming her body with his. His emotions surprised him, the rage he felt at Virgil, his strong desire to comfort her. He'd so wanted to look into the crowd and find her there, waiting to see him.

You're dreaming, buddy. You're no more important to her than the rest of the parade.

But she circled his waist and held on as if he was an anchor on a storm-tossed sea. Scared was all. He hoped she did not feel the thundering of his heartbeat as he held her close.

Jingles sat watching, tail wagging, the candy cane still clenched between his teeth.

When she recovered enough to pull away from him, her autumn eyes gleamed with determination. She exhaled before she spoke, a long and steady breath. "Virgil thinks I know where the jewelry is. He offered a deal. He said he'd erase the video and drop the charges if I hand it over."

"And if you don't?"

"He will kill Tammy and me."

Liam fought down another swell of rage as he watched her. He wouldn't blame her for taking the easy way out. No negotiating with terrorists was always a fine policy until the lives of loved ones hung in the balance. She wasn't a solider trained to fight or even a cowboy used to physical struggle on a daily basis. He waited to see if Maggie Lofton would reveal what she was really made of.

She breathed out again, took off her scarf and jammed it into her pocket. He saw the angry red blotches on her throat. "Even if I had the

Hope Diamond in my pocket, I wouldn't give it to Virgil in a million years."

He grinned, his spirit bubbling to match the river of fire in hers. "Excellent. I got your back, Maggie. We all do."

Without warning she kissed him, catching the corner of his mouth. "Thank you, Cowboy Santa."

He ducked his head and sought her mouth then, his pulse pounding as his lips found hers. A jolt of sweetness rippled through him, like the pure joy of a perfect sunrise. It was only a moment before they both backed away. "You're, uh, welcome," he managed to say.

"You... I mean, I appreciate what you're doing for Tammy."

He admitted to himself then that his motivation to help his ex-girlfriend's sister had turned into something completely different. Tammy and Maggie might be sisters, but they occupied completely different places in his mind and heart. But Maggie didn't need to know that and he wouldn't add to her discomfort by sharing it. He was just a guy lending a hand because of his history with Tammy. Friends, at best.

Off-limits.

That's how she thought of him.

Or maybe damaged goods? The dark thought

made him look away, toward the spectators that were beginning to thin out. *Steady on, Liam.*

When he turned back, she was pulling a business card from her jeans' pocket. "I ran into Yoriko. She's a friend of my sister's. She said Tammy visited her on Wednesday and left something."

Liam whistled. "Good detective work. I'll stable Streak and we can drive right over there."

"Monday," Maggie said. "She told me to come then."

"All right. Let's go to the ranch, someplace quiet and safe, and call Danny. There's probably some leftovers we can snag."

She raised an eyebrow. "Isn't Aunt Ginny feeding you well enough?"

"Sure, but there's always room for a pancake."

He'd coaxed the smile from her that he'd intended. She was still scared, but not shaking anymore.

If Virgil Salvador thought he could threaten Maggie's sister and get away with it, he had another think coming. And if he thought he'd intimidated Maggie by his little stunt at the parade, he was in for one big, bad surprise.

THIRTEEN

There were no further Virgil sightings, so the next day Liam was determined to keep Maggie as close as possible.

In spite of his state of alert, he enjoyed the Sunday church service more than ever. Perhaps it was the beautiful holly arrangements that festooned the altar, or maybe sitting next to Charlie before he toddled off to Sunday school. Maybe it was seeing Mitch holding Jane's hand, her head resting on his shoulder. It was also possible it was because Maggie sat on his other side, close enough that he could catch the clean scent of her shampoo and admire the graceful line of her profile while she listened to the message. He'd spent the prior evening eating pancakes in the ranch kitchen and escorting her to the saddlery.

"There's no need to be my personal bodyguard," she'd said.

He'd cheerfully ignored her. "I'm just in it for the pancakes," he joked. At her doubtful expression, he'd put a finger gently on her bruised throat. "And he's not going to touch you again."

After church he drove Maggie to the Chuck-wagon where they'd arranged to meet Mitch, Chad, Tammy, Joe and his sister. When they arrived, Maggie insisted on helping Nan for a few minutes.

Once again he settled into a corner table with a slice of pie and a cup of coffee where he could keep her in his line of sight. He admired the way she whirled through the kitchen, popping up at the window, her cheeks pink with the warmth. She looked completely at ease, naturally re-laxed, the way he felt in the saddle or roving the grassy hills on Streak. It all looked so fluid, effortless. She was an artist in her domain, just like he was with his leather and knives, fashion-ing something amazing and useful. He was al-most certain when he ate her pancakes he could taste the love she put into them, her tender spirit. His nonsensical fancies evaporated as Mitch slid into a chair opposite him, following his line of sight. "Keeping close tabs on her?"

"Uh-huh."

Mitch sat in silence until Liam couldn't stand it. "What?"

Mitch shrugged, a wisp of a smile on his lips. "Nothing."

"Not nothing."

"Just thinking you and Maggie seem to get along well."

"Friends."

"Uh-huh."

"Seriously."

"Uh-huh."

He thunked his mug on the table. "She's Tammy's sister. There's a rule about dating siblings, you know."

Mitch accepted a cup of coffee from the waitress and slugged some down. "So you're not supposed to love her."

"Right."

"I get it. Not supposed to love your brother's ex, either."

Liam stopped mid-retort, gaping. He'd not considered recently how much Mitch had probably struggled over a relationship with his killer brother's former spouse. That relationship had busted the rule book wide-open.

Mitch laughed. "Took me a while to get over those rules, too." He paused. "I'm glad I did, or I wouldn't have Jane and Charlie in my life."

Liam had no idea what to say so he closed his mouth, relieved when Mitch took out his phone. "Got some intel for you on Virgil."

Just then Tammy and Joe arrived and saw them. Joe pulled out a chair for Tammy, which earned him some points with Liam, before seating himself. Maggie noticed them and Liam rose and slid out a chair for her when she came over.

She sat. "There's a lull in the action, so I'm taking a ten-minute break."

Tammy laughed. "Right. Let's see if you can actually sit for a whole ten minutes before you rush right back into that kitchen."

Maggie shrugged. "It seemed like you were all settling in for some serious talking and I didn't want to miss anything."

"Got some intel." Mitch slid a look at Joe and then back at Liam. As much as Liam felt like keeping the information "in the family," as he liked to say, Joe was a part of the equation.

"Tell us what you found out," he urged his brother.

"Virgil's a smart guy. Helped his father run a commercial laundry business in Cambria. Used to visit his uncle Bill and worked the farm in the summers."

"He mentioned that to me once or twice," Joe said. "Always seemed nostalgic about those summers."

"Uncle Bill said Virgil made some great suggestions on how to manage the feed business. The sad thing is, Uncle Bill loves Virgil, I think. His own son passed away in a plane crash in his early forties.

"Leaving behind the granddaughter, Vivian,

to whom Bill has deeded the property in his will. I checked that one out. It's legit. She has three kids, lives in France, husband left her for greener pastures after her youngest child was born a couple of months ago."

Tammy grimaced. "Stand-up guy."

Mitch continued. "Virgil's dad's business went belly-up when he was in high school. His mother, Harriet, didn't take it well. She became an alcoholic."

Joe nodded. "He said his mom couldn't abide how her brother-in-law lorded it over them. Said Bill was a greedy Scrooge who wouldn't help them."

"That's not the Bill I know," Tammy said.

"Somewhere in the middle usually lies the truth," Mitch said. "Probably came as a shock to Virgil when Bill changed his will to leave his property to Vivian. I have a call in to her."

Mitch drank more coffee. "Virgil thinks of himself as a ladies' man. I spoke to his ex-girl-friend, who laughed at me for calling her that. She said she went out with him twice before he proposed. She laughed at him, too. Said he's delusional."

Joe's mouth pinched into a tight line. "He wanted Tammy for himself."

Tammy looked at the tabletop. "It was em-barrassing. I loved my job, but he wouldn't stop pestering me. I had to flat-out tell him I would never go out with him. I still don't think he believed me."

Joe grimaced. "When I started dating Tammy, I stopped working for Bill. It became too weird to have Virgil ogling her when I was standing right there." He wrapped his arm around her shoulder. "It's okay. I've found a little contract work to keep me afloat. I tried to end things cordially with Virgil as best I could." He blinked hard. "If I had known he would threaten you, I never would have—" He broke off.

Tammy smiled. "It's okay. I got you out of the deal."

Joe squeezed her. "I'm no prize."

"Yes, you are. You're a hardworking, gentle-mannered guy who's shared everything with me. I feel like I know your whole family."

Liam felt a hitch in his breathing. He felt no jealousy toward what Joe and Tammy had, only regret that he was not the kind of guy who could pour out his life, his fear, so easily. He hadn't made a go of it with Tammy. That was okay, since he did not feel they'd been meant for each other, but as his gaze shifted to Maggie, he worried that he would never be able to share everything with her, or any woman. The past was better kept there, and his monstrous fear about the future was too great a burden for anyone else.

"All right," Liam said. "Virgil's probably in debt, from what we've heard, and angry that he was cheated out of what he feels is rightfully his, and happy to hang Tammy out to dry. Thanks for the intel, Mitch. I take it you discovered all this without Danny's help?"

Mitch shrugged. "I'll share it with him. Cops are used to getting the crumbs after the Marshals dig up the good stuff."

"Spoken like a former US marshal," Liam said with a chuckle.

Maggie's phone rang. She frowned at the screen. "I don't know this number." She punched the button and immediately her face went slack with fear.

Liam grabbed the phone and pressed it to his good ear. It still wasn't loud enough, so he activated the speaker and thumbed the volume all the way up. "Virgil, is that you?"

His voice vibrated with anger. "You had no right—none at all—to contact my girlfriend. She texted me to tell me she's changing her number because she wants nothing more to do with me."

Time to bait the bear. "That's old news," Liam said. "She told you to buzz off long ago.

As a matter of fact, she says she never was your girlfriend in the first place."

The line went silent but Liam imagined he could feel the rage billowing through the airwaves.

"Stop poking around in my life—all of you!" Virgil seethed.

"We're going to keep on poking and prodding and pestering until you wind up in jail where you belong," Liam said.

"I'm not going to jail, and you just made a deadly mistake."

"Leave Maggie and Tammy alone, Virgil. That's my advice to you. Take it." He heard nothing else, realizing, when the others all sat back in their chairs, that Virgil must have disconnected.

"Well, well," he said. "Looks like we rattled a cage, now, didn't we?"

Maggie's hands were clenched on the tabletop and he perceived he shouldn't have added to her fear by goading Virgil. "I'm not going to let him hurt you," he said quietly. "I'm right at your side through this whole thing, and maybe we can make some progress tomorrow."

"What's tomorrow?" Tammy asked, struggling to her feet on her hobbled ankle.

Liam told them about their visit to Yoriko.

"Watch your backs," Mitch said.

"Yes, big brother." Liam watched Maggie return to the kitchen, her agitation clear in her rapid strides. *And I'll watch hers, too.*

Maggie wanted to lose herself in the kitchen. She was happy to stay on and help with the dinner shift, in spite of Liam's concern. There seemed to be nothing she could do anyway, until they visited Yoriko.

"I need the money," she said to Liam. "The Corvette needs a new set of tires if Tammy's going to keep driving it."

"I know someone who can change the tires for you real cheap."

"So do I," Maggie said. "Me."

He jerked. "Your sister doesn't even know how to open the hood."

"I'm not my sister."

Something soft and sweet and tender crept into his gaze. "That's for sure," he mumbled.

She felt suddenly awkward at his frank stare. "I've been working on cars since I was six. Anyway, they need my help until seven. The Corvette is parked out back, so I can drive myself to the ranch."

"Nice try. I'll be back before then. Gotta meet the farrier to reshoe Streak. Chad's going to take a shift here, then Mitch, and I'll be back after that. Don't leave until I'm here, okay?"

There was no sense in arguing.

She finally got him out the door and returned to the stove where Tiny was bellowing out a song about boats and lost love.

"You're a romantic at heart, Tiny," she said.

"Romance and ravioli," he said, waving a slotted spoon. "That's the life for me." He winked at her. "You could do with a dash of romance in your life, too, you know. That cowboy might just fit the bill."

She waved him away with a spatula. Romance. Who had time for that? Certainly she had more practical things to do with her time than think about Liam Pike. Her days and months and years had been spent on the two things she loved the most: cooking and her family. Sure there were friends and the occasional date, but romance was just something she hadn't made space for and it was certainly not the right time for it now.

The hours passed in a satisfying blur of chicken potpies, steaks, fries, cheeseburgers and pasta. When the dinner rush eased, the kitchen staff breathed a collective sigh of relief. Thoroughly tired and satisfied, Maggie met Liam at the back door.

"Mmm," he said, leaning close, "what's that perfume you're wearing? Au de cheeseburger?"

"That's the one."

"I like it," he said.

Laughing, Maggie followed him out to the dark parking lot. She opened the driver's-side door and slid inside the Corvette.

Liam stopped dead.

Her skin went cold. "What?"

"Do you smell that?"

She sniffed the air. "It smells like gasoline." Only it was not a faint aroma, she realized, but a pungent odor that filled the air.

He took her hand. "Get out of the car—"

He hadn't finished his sentence when a metallic squeaking over his shoulder caught her attention. Someone was standing on the roof of the metal shed that housed the extra restaurant supplies, overlooking the parking lot. She could not see who it was since a hood covered the hair and the lot was lit only by one dirt-encrusted light. Squinting, she saw a glint as the person moved, slowly and stealthily.

"Liam," she whispered.

But he had not heard the man. He was pulling at her to get out.

She tugged at his sleeve and pointed. "Up there."

Just as he swiveled around to follow her direction, the man's arm went up in the air and a yellow flame spurted to life. The light from the flare momentarily dazzled her vision.

Her mind put together the pieces. Gasoline…

flame… She watched in horror as the stranger hurled the flare, a sputtering streak of gold, directly toward her.

Liam saw the flicker of flame mirrored in Maggie's eyes. The light arced in a shower of gold as the struck flare plummeted through the night. He hauled her clear just as it impacted the top of the Corvette. The impact was absorbed by the whoosh when the gasoline caught.

He ran with her a safe distance, then stopped and searched her face. "Are you hurt? Burned?"

She shook her head, face white with shock, but she was racked by coughs and part of her sleeve had burned away, probably taking some of her skin with it.

There was no way he was going to capture the arsonist who, he was certain, had to be Virgil. Flames crawled over the doused roof of the car, rippling down over the sides. It was a matter of keeping Maggie and everyone else safe and putting out the fire before it had a chance to catch the stacked pallets or other vehicles.

He pushed her back. "Go inside and call 9-1-1. I've got a fire extinguisher in my truck."

By now Tiny had puffed his way out the back door. Helen was just behind him, holding a notepad, probably interrupted in the act of working out a dessert order since the Lodge outsourced their sweets to the Chuckwagon.

"Take Maggie inside," Liam called to her.

Helen immediately nodded and took Maggie by the hand.

He grabbed the extinguisher from his truck and pressed the nozzle to get the foam started. The flames had licked down to the ground, finding the puddles of gasoline poured under the car. The fire propelled outward in a circle of orange and blue. Liam was able to leap backward quickly enough to avoid the onslaught, but acrid smoke infiltrated his lungs, stinging his eyes. He advanced again, aiming the extinguisher in a futile effort. The car would not be salvageable, but he might still keep the fire under control until the fire department arrived. The wail of a siren became distinct, closer with each passing minute.

Liam was not ready for the blast of the front two tires exploding in quick succession. The noise seemed to pop something inside his head, but he continued to press on. Another diner added his fire extinguisher to the fight and, for a few moments, Liam continued. Slowly, incrementally, a horrifying realization pushed to the surface. The foam from the extinguisher made no noise as it spurted through the nozzle. Liam stared as the reality hammered home.

The world had gone silent.

He looked at the flames. Though he knew the engulfed vehicle was crackling and popping as the fire consumed it, he could not hear a single sound. It was as if he was watching a film without the audio. Feverishly he checked to ensure the hearing aid was still in his ear. Stomach sinking, he realized it was. The problem was not the device.

The exploding tires had made an instant reality of the thing Liam feared most. Panic knotted his insides, traced an invisible fire through his body. He wanted nothing more than to run, to sprint away into the darkness, but he would not leave, not until he knew Maggie was safe. Numbly he sprayed on until the fire department arrived with Danny Patron hot on its heels.

Maggie was led to the back of an ambulance. She seemed to be moving well, but they would take her to be checked out anyway, the burn on her arm treated. Lights strobed the night as the ambulance pulled away from the Chuckwagon.

Liam dropped the extinguisher and backed away. Danny came close and Liam saw that he was talking, but he could not make out even one tiny syllable.

Danny finally grabbed his arm. "…wrong?"

Liam could read that one word on Danny's lips.

Puzzlement changed to concern, but Liam

could not stay. He practically ran to his truck, shoved the key into the ignition and felt the engine rumble to life. He was about to jerk the truck into gear when Helen ran to his window, her lips moving with a question he did not need to hear to understand. When he rolled down the window her fingers grabbed his sleeve, tight enough to dig into his arm. She stared into his eyes and he shook his head.

"I can't hear," he said.

She held on, probably telling him to stay, to go to the doctor, to share his terror. But he couldn't. It was thundering through him, unmanning and infusing him with the most terrifying loneliness he'd ever felt, worse than when his mother died, darker than his father's descent into the well of depression, more frightening than being under fire in Afghanistan.

"I have to go to the hospital with Maggie," he said again, not even sure if he was speaking loud enough. He pulled his arm from her grip, put the truck into gear and sped out of the parking lot and into the night.

FOURTEEN

Maggie was surprised, when she finally finished with the doctor, that Liam was nowhere to be found. Helen ushered her to an SUV, brushing aside her questions about Liam. Maggie's knees had stopped shaking, but her nerves were still alight with adrenaline and a low, simmering anger. Imagining the wreck of the burned-out Corvette, her sister's pride and joy, made her cringe, but not with fear anymore. In the course of telling Danny Patron, her thoughts and fear had crystallized into a sense of outrage.

Virgil was angry at their investigation of him. He'd threatened punishment and he'd delivered by almost burning her alive. Danny Patron was on his way to Bill Salvador's home to track him down. Maggie did not have much hope that it would be a fruitful trip. Virgil was too clever.

Helen was moving so fast, Maggie could almost not keep up with her. "Where is Liam?" she asked.

Helen looked away. "He stayed at the hospital until they assured him you were unharmed. Then Danny wanted his statement. He's there now, I think."

"I was surprised he hadn't texted me."

"Um, he's not himself right now, but he would want me to take you home. You've had a terrible time."

Muscles tightened along her spine and Maggie stopped in front of the car door to face Helen. "Is Liam hurt? Was he injured trying to put out the fire? Tell me."

Helen shook her head, a muscle jumping in her jaw. "No. Get in, Maggie. Please."

Maggie obeyed.

Helen guided the car along the same road where Maggie had almost crashed into the train.

"What happened to Liam?" she repeated.

"He wouldn't want me to…" Helen shook her head. "He's really upset."

"You know I care about him. What's more, he's in this situation because of Tammy and me. Please, Helen. I want to help him."

Helen gave her a sidelong glance before answering. "I think when the tires exploded… I mean…" She swallowed and tried again. "The sound deafened him." The last words came out shaky. "Completely."

Maggie gasped. "Is it temporary? A doctor…"

"I don't know. He's scared, Maggie. Terrified." Her voice wobbled but she forced out another breath. "He's never allowed himself to be scared, you see. What happened to us as kids changed him. Did he tell you any of it?"

Maggie nodded. "Only a little. That your mom died and your father stopped being a parent to you."

A half smile drifted over Helen's mouth. "Liam must really care for you, too, if he shared that."

Maggie did not know what to say, but she knew she was blushing in the darkness. People who cared about each other shared, didn't they? So why wouldn't he trust her?

Helen continued. "My mom died in an auto accident caused because my father was reaching for a water bottle and he took his eyes off the road. Dad could never get over it. He blamed himself. He became severely depressed and he couldn't function, for the most part. He refused to see a therapist or get help."

"How old were you?"

"I was five. Liam was seven. Liam learned… I mean, he must have been scared, just a little boy, but he learned to be in charge, to pretend everything was fine when my dad was incapacitated. He fooled teachers, social workers, everybody. I think he even fooled himself, after a while, into thinking he didn't need anybody's help. I wish I could tell you how amazing Liam is, Maggie. He's been the best brother, and he always put me first. Always." She blinked back tears. "In high school, he wanted so desperately to play baseball, but he got a job instead at the grocery store to pay our bills."

"Oh," Maggie sighed. "How sweet."

"My senior year he sold his pocketknife so I could have a dress for prom." A tear trickled down Helen's cheek. "He loved that knife." She laughed. "Except that he must have threatened my date with a heinous fate if he touched me, because the guy was afraid even to pin on my corsage."

Maggie smiled but pain cleaved through her thinking about that child, Liam, forced into the role of a grown-up, father, brother, protector, pretender.

"So he laughs and jokes to the world but inside he feels things deeply and now…" Helen sniffled. "He's so scared and alone. He won't even share it with me."

Maggie gripped her arm. "What can I do? How can I help?"

Helen pulled onto the ranch property and delivered Maggie to the door of the saddlery. "I don't know. I pray every night that God would show me how to reach him or send somebody else who could."

There in the car, Helen cried for a little while and Maggie sat with her, heart breaking for both Helen and her brother. She prayed aloud and comforted as best she could until Helen was calmer.

When she drove away, Maggie let herself into the saddlery and tried to shower off the stench of smoke. Sleep was out of the question. She'd almost been burned alive. Tammy's car had been obliterated and she should be anticipating word from Danny Patron, but all she could think about was Liam.

Her texts to him went unanswered. She strolled along the length of his worktable, fingers trailing over the supple scraps. In the corner was a tiny leather dog, Jingles; she could tell by the crooked paws and goofy grin. It must be the ornament he was making for Helen's Christmas tree. She set him carefully back in the corner as if he, too, was waiting for Liam's return.

The clock ticked away the hours and finally she settled into a chair, dozing, until she awakened just after midnight, heart thudding as memories of the burning car tumbled through her thoughts. She went to the window, peeking at the bunkhouse and wondering if Liam's truck was there. Frost covered the window, glazing the black fields, backlit by a plump moon. A spot of white gleamed in the gloom. Peering closer, her breath caught. Liam was leaning against the split rail fence, his forehead pressed to his arms. Jingles sat at his feet, staring loyally at his silent master.

Indecision cut a path inside her. Maggie had made it a habit to stay away from relationships with people outside of her family. She was friendly, helpful, cordial, but she could not recall a time when she'd involved herself in another person's life in the way she contemplated now. Could there be a worse time, when Liam's whole spirit was splayed open to pain and hopelessness? When he clearly wanted nothing to do with her? What could she say? How could she help? There was nothing she could do and the thought of trying pricked her with goose bumps.

But his profile was so defeated, the strong shoulders bowed with a weight that must be agony to bear alone. Helen…she should call Helen. Surely his sister would be the right helpmate, not her, not Maggie, not a person who spent more time with pasta than people. She reached for the phone when she felt the command blooming inside.

Go.

After a shaky breath, she let the strong urge take hold of her and, before she could talk herself out of it, she propelled herself out the door.

He didn't look up at her approach, but Jingles

did. The dog whined and danced tiny steps back and forth between her and Liam as if to say, "Help him. Fix him."

Liam's slight shift told her he was aware of her presence. She moved next to him. He must have been standing there for a long time, since tiny ice crystals had begun to collect on his barn jacket. He smelled of acrid smoke. For a moment she gazed out at the moonlit fields, putting away her clamoring thoughts and doubts and letting her God-given instincts take over.

She reached for his hand, ice-cold against hers. He did not take hers, but neither did he flinch away, his face still buried in his arm. She pulled at his hand until he was forced back from the fence to face her. But his gaze was riveted on the ground. Streaks showed where he had cried, the tears washing away some of the soot from the fire.

"I…" he said, the words dying at his feet.

She gripped his fingers and guided him to the main house. He was slow, stumbling almost, but she moved patiently. When Liam stopped, Jingles stopped, too, sitting quietly until Liam was ready to move again. The door was unlocked, as it always was, she'd learned earlier, and the house was quiet and still. She led him to a leather sofa and pushed him down onto it. Then she tipped his chin up with her finger.

"Stay here. I'll be right back." She whispered the words slowly, and he watched her lips hungrily as if wishing with all his strength that he could hear her.

She got what she needed from the kitchen: a bowl and warm water. Kneeling in front of him, she took off his hat and washed the soot from his face. He withstood her ministrations, shivering as he gradually warmed, his eyes roving her face as she worked. When the soot was rinsed away, she returned the items to the kitchen and prepared them both a mug of hot tea.

She sat next to him, shoes off, feet curled up on the cushion, and they drank. When his eyes began to grow heavy, she took the mug from his grasp and wrapped a blanket around him. He looked at her then, defeat showing clear even in the dim lamplight. He started to speak then stopped. She nodded encouragement and Jingles gave the knee of his jeans a lick.

"I can't hear," he whispered. "Anything." The brokenness made her desperate.

She cupped his face with her palms and stroked his cheeks until the hopelessness subsided, she thought, just a fraction. She could not help, she could not fix, or nourish, or comfort much, but she would be there with Liam as long as he needed her to be, and God would enable

her to tell him that he was not alone, even if he
could not hear the words.

"It's okay," she whispered. "It's going to be
okay."

"You almost died."

"I'm right here."

When his eyes closed and his head fell back
on the cushions, she settled the blanket more
firmly around him and then fixed herself another cup of tea, keeping the lamp on to drive
the shadows away.

Liam awakened, disoriented, his temples
aching. His blurry vision cleared enough so he
could discern he was in the main house. It must
be early, predawn. Maggie was curled up in the
chair across from him, cheek on her arm, asleep
in the lamplight. Jingles sprawled on the throw
rug, nose twitching in sleep.

He tried to make sense of it. Maggie had
stayed with him all night. His memory dredged
up the feel of her washing his face, stroking his
cheeks, her calm certainty. Shame and wonder
twined inside him and drove him to his feet. He
stood there, breathing hard, reliving her gentle
touch and the look in her eyes. It hadn't been
pity, had it? He could not stand the thought that
she pitied him, but how could she not? She'd
led him to the house like a lost child, washing

his face and fixing him tea. Liam could handle anything that life dished out to him, but not to be an object of sympathy, especially not by a woman as amazing as Maggie. It was too much. He headed for the door. Jingles awakened, yawned widely and trotted after him with a shake of his collar.

"Quiet, dog," he muttered. "You'll wake the whole household." And that's when it blazed in his brain like a thunderbolt. His hearing had returned, at least some of it. He practically ran outside and snapped his fingers next to his good ear. The sound was dull and he still heard a persistent pulsing, a by-product of the explosion, but whatever part of his auditory system still functioned picked up his snapping fingers sure as shooting. Elation surged through him. He could still hear, at least for the time being.

He thanked God as he walked to the bunkhouse, trying to corral his ricocheting emotions. Chad and Mitch both stopped midsentence when he arrived, eyeballing him from the porch.

"Wasn't sure you were going to be up for chores today," Mitch said cautiously.

Liam's face heated. "Helen called?"

Chad exchanged a relieved look with Mitch and nodded. "Many times since last night. She told us Maggie is okay but you were incommunicado. Hearing's back, huh?"

He had to answer with a nod since he did not trust himself to reply.

Mitch clapped him on the back. "That's what Jane and I were praying for, and Aunt Ginny and Uncle Gus. The whole family."

He wanted to make a joke, a wisecrack, anything to deflect the weighty emotion of the moment, but he found he could not. "I'm grateful," he mumbled.

"Us, too," Chad said. They stood for a moment in silence and once again Liam thanked God for his family and for their stalwart faith.

"Got a report from Danny."

Liam almost sighed in relief. Mitch knew that Liam needed to get back on solid ground, to step away from the unpredictable feelings that ballooned inside him. His heart swelled with unspoken thanks as he listened to his brother.

"Virgil's got an alibi," Mitch said with a head shake.

"What?" Liam exploded, a surge of pain reminding him he had a headache. "How can that be?"

"Pizza delivery guy says he made a drop to Virgil Salvador at Bill's house during the time the Corvette was burning. Before you ask, Virgil paid cash, so there's no receipt proof. He said his doorbell camera was offline so he can't provide proof that way, but the pizza kid gave a statement."

"Obviously he paid the kid to lie for him."

"Probably."

Liam groaned then jerked a look at his cell phone. "I almost forgot. We have to go see Yoriko today, after chores. She said Tammy left something with her. Maybe it will help us turn up the heat on Virgil. If nothing else, it will mess up his insurance scam. He's gonna go down one way or the other." Saying the words made him feel better, stronger.

Chad scratched his eyebrow. "I got time. I can do your chores."

Liam went hot again. "No need. I'm fine. Can't get to Yoriko's until afternoon anyway. I will tell Aunt Ginny and Uncle Gus to keep Maggie close until we go." And he hoped the delay would give him some time to figure out how he was going to approach Maggie. After he'd practically run away like a kid afraid of the bogeyman, he'd have to come up with just the right way to play it to try to reverse what she was no doubt thinking of him.

"Fine," Mitch said, "you can help me secure the heifer that needs her second dose of meds, but before you do anything else, call your sister."

"It's too early."

Mitch shook his head, looking every bit as intimidating as he no doubt appeared during his days as a US marshal. "You're calling her now and I'm going to brief Aunt Ginny and Uncle Gus on your current status."

"But…"

"Now," he said.

Chad gave him a "better you than me" smile and disappeared into the bunkhouse.

Liam sighed, turned the volume all the way up on his phone and thought about what kind of quip or joke he could possibly rustle up to let his sister know he was okay.

He was still swamped with the memory of the previous night, isolated, cocooned in silence and terror, when Maggie had sat with him, a steady, comforting presence. Somehow he'd known then that with her he would be okay. It no longer seemed to matter in the least that she was Tammy's sister. She was all tender hands and heart, keeping him tethered with her calm faith. His pulse beat faster at the thought.

And what was it exactly that he'd felt in the strange hours the night before? How could he have such deep feelings for her? The thoughts twisted around inside him. He had cared for other women in his lifetime, or at least thought he had, but never like this. Never had he allowed someone like Maggie to make it through his sturdy walls.

But what kind of man was he for her? A child who needed his face washed and his hand held?

He remembered boiling water for pasta, a ten-year-old boy who could barely reach the stove. He'd left a pot holder too near the burner and it caught fire, the flames spreading to the empty macaroni and cheese box. He'd dumped the whole pot of water and pasta on the flames and doused them, but he remembered his fear when the fire had licked and sputtered its way toward the curtain. He'd tried to hide his terror from Helen when she'd entered the kitchen after smelling the smoke, assuring her he had it all under control, when he'd really just felt like running away from the burgeoning flames.

Running away, just like he'd done when he finished with the cops and the hospital. What kind of partner would flee like a scalded cat from what scared him the most instead of stand and face it? Shame tore him up inside. He had no more time to think about it as his sister picked up on the first ring.

FIFTEEN

Maggie awoke in the ranch house only to be fussed over by Ginny and Gus. Liam called, leaving messages to check on her, but she sent a quick text to reassure him rather than call him back. The thought of seeing Liam again made her pulse skitter after what had happened the night before. Finally, when she could stand being cooped up no longer, she hitched a ride to town with Uncle Gus, in spite of Ginny's efforts to persuade her to stay. At least at the Lodge she might be able to see Helen and talk to her sister.

Gus made jovial conversation during the drive until they pulled up at their destination. "Liam said to tell you he'd be clear of his duties soon," Gus said.

"Thank you. I'll be ready. I'm sorry you had to do escort duty."

"No problem. Happy to do it."

He stopped her exit from the truck with a touch on her sleeve.

"Ginny and I wanted to thank you, for taking care of our boy Liam last night."

Maggie started. "How did you know? Did Liam tell you?"

He chuckled. "No way. Liam would never tell us anything so personal. Ginny came downstairs to check on things and saw you, so she hightailed it right out of there. Got the follow-up from Mitch."

"Liam doesn't like to share."

"Could be God just didn't put the right person in his path before." Gus smiled. "Someone strong enough to hold together his broken pieces. That's what my Ginny is to me." The love in his expression softened his age lines, rolled the years away, so she saw him as the dashing cowboy he must have been, and still was. "She knew I was a cracked pot when she first met me and she married me anyway. Isn't that something?" He winked at her. "Now you and Liam be careful today, huh? We've had plenty of drama already."

Maggie got out, pondering as she entered the festive lobby. Someone strong enough to hold together the broken pieces? She'd never been strong enough nor willing to do that for anyone except her twin and her parents. Was God leading her to do that for Liam? *You can't give your heart to someone who doesn't want it*, she told herself savagely.

Maggie spotted Tammy immediately, sitting in a cozy armchair by the fire, with Joe next to her. Tammy jumped up and hugged Maggie when she joined them. "You could have been killed, or Liam," she whispered.

"He's not going to get away with it." She forced her sister to sit again, noting that she'd become far too thin. "Have you been eating enough?"

"Never mind that," Tammy said, exasperated. "You almost got burned up last night."

"Don't overdramatize." Maggie sighed. "But your gorgeous Corvette…"

Tammy poked her ribs. "I don't care about the car, you ninny. Virgil's pulling out all the stops now. I'm scared."

Joe nodded. "He's desperate. He wants that jewelry, and he'll kill one of you to force the other sister into giving it to him."

"We've got to get our hands on it," Tammy said. "If only I could remember."

"The memories will return," Joe said. "And once we find the jewels, there won't be any more need for him to come after you."

Tammy swallowed. "At the police station he said he'd release the video, but that might not be enough now. Maybe he won't be satisfied until we pay in blood."

"I'm confident it won't come to that." Maggie forced a smile over the rush of worry.

Joe lowered his voice. "I heard Danny Patron say the insurance company will make a decision by Christmas. If the jewelry doesn't turn up, they'll pay out. It's adding urgency for Virgil."

Maggie recalled Virgil's fingers punching through the material of her scarf, pulling it tight around her neck.

Tammy's jaw clenched, and she shook her head. "I have to find Bill's diamonds. He needs them back and Virgil's not going to get what he wants."

Joe stroked her arm reassuringly. "That's why we've been going over and over Tammy's movements, trying to remember where she might have left it, but things are still real fuzzy."

"Going to Yoriko's today," Maggie said. "Maybe that will tell us something."

Tammy's brow furrowed in thought. "She's a glassblower. I met her last Christmas when I lived here. We're friends." She chewed her lip. "She lives on the coast about an hour from here, between Driftwood and Sand Dune. She has a little shop, too, but I don't remember visiting her recently." She rubbed her head. "Everything's still all jumbled in my mind and I can't get rid of this headache."

"That's okay. I'll go see what I can turn up," Maggie said.

"I'm coming with you," Tammy said.

"No way," Maggie and Joe said at the same time.

Maggie smiled at her sister's frustration. "Liam's coming. I won't be alone."

Joe stood. "And there's no way you should be doing any sleuthing after what Virgil did. You're safest here with me. Besides, your ankle is still swollen. As a matter of fact, I'm going to get you an ice pack." He kissed her and walked away.

Tammy smiled. "He's good to me."

"I never would have thought you'd pair up with a computer programmer."

She laughed. "You sound like Liam. Neither did I, but Joe balances out my wild side. He loves to take care of me. He's told me everything about his life. He's the only boy in a family of five girls. Can you believe it? The baby, yet. I think he never got a chance to be in charge of anything until he moved out." Tammy cocked her chin. "I hope you find someone like that, Mags, a guy who loves to take care of you." Her look went sly. "Or maybe you already have?"

"What?"

"I saw the way Liam looked at you in the restaurant."

Maggie felt the flush creep up her neck. "Oh,

it's just all the weird circumstances. There's nothing between us. He's..."

"My ex-boyfriend?" Tammy said.

"Well, yeah."

"And we liked each other, but that wasn't enough of a connection for me. He would perpetually steer clear of sharing too much. There was always a sort of hesitation in him. But I think you two have something different."

"We don't have anything at all." Maggie knocked her foot on the coffee table, nearly upsetting Tammy's mug of tea. "I mean, he's just helping out because you two dated and he's a good guy."

"No," she said, shaking her head. "That's not why he's hanging around. Not entirely anyway."

Maggie squirmed. "I have to go, Tam. I should see if Helen needs anyone to help in the kitchen."

"Always got your work to protect you, huh, Mags?"

Irritation flashed through her. "Work is what keeps our family afloat, in case you didn't notice. Pays my bills and sometimes yours."

"I have noticed, and I appreciate it, Maggie. I'm just saying—"

Maggie cut her off. "If we're ever going to reopen Dad's restaurant..."

"Dad wouldn't want you to miss out on your

own dreams while trying to breathe life back into his. He's told you as much."

Now the irritation flipped to anger. "It's my dream, too."

Tammy reached up and grabbed Maggie's hand. "I know, and I am so proud of your work ethic and how you've been the rock of our family, even when I was busy shipwrecking myself. You are selfless, more than I could ever be, but sometimes I worry that your work is a way to keep out other messier things that God might want you to experience."

Maggie let out a breath and kissed Tammy. "I love you, sis."

"I love you, too, Mags, and I just want you to know, if there was anything developing between you and Liam…that would be totally fine with me."

Maggie grinned in spite of herself. "What happened to the 'sisters' exes are completely off-limits' rule?"

She shrugged. "You could stand to break a few rules, little sister."

"Says the person two whole minutes older than me." Their laughter mingled with the cheerful hum of the lobby.

Maggie said goodbye and headed for the door, thinking about broken pieces and broken rules.

That's not why he's hanging around. Not entirely anyway.

She hoped the kitchen would help her sort out the muddle in her heart and head.

At two o'clock Liam was showered, dressed in jeans and a clean T-shirt under his barn jacket. He wore his second-best cowboy hat since his other had been blackened in the Chuckwagon parking lot. His hands were cold, his stomach tight as he waited for Maggie in the lobby of the Lodge.

Start with a joke? A thank-you nestled in some self-deprecating comment?

She wore a green shirt under her jean jacket and it set off the cream of her skin and reflected the iridescent green glimmer in her eyes. He swallowed hard, remembering her cupping his cheeks, watching him, washing his face, anchoring him. He yearned to forget those hours, but at the same time he desperately wanted to hold them close, to hold her close. What was wrong with him?

Plastering on a relaxed expression, he shoved his hat back and greeted her with a jaunty grin. "Managed to secure Jingles this time at the bunkhouse. Filled up the hole he dug under the gate."

"That was a good trick."

"Yeah, well, he's like some sort of Houdini and, no matter what I do, he seems to turn up."

Maggie nodded. "I spoke to Tammy and Joe." She related her conversation with them. He listened and responded. A question here, a comment there, and then the conversation sputtered and died like a match dropped into a puddle.

"So, um, are you, feeling okay?" he asked as he led her to the truck and helped her in.

"Yes. Just a minor burn on my arm. Losing the Vette was sad."

"Tragic," he agreed. "That was one sweet machine, but you're far more important than any car." Again the silence became awkward between them and he felt the weight of her gaze. There was no more avoiding the elephant that sat between them. Might as well saddle up and ride the ungainly thing. "So uh, thank you, for what you did last night. I mean, I was sort of freaked out, but I shouldn't have been such a toddler about it. Charlie probably would have handled it better." He tried for a laugh, which sounded hollow. "Guess I worried everyone, especially Helen…and you."

She put her hand over the top of his where it lay on the seat. "You were scared, Liam. You don't have to be ashamed about feeling that way, or sharing it with me."

He didn't? No shame about baring his deepest insecurity and fear? All of a sudden he was a seven-year-old boy again, putting on his father's coat, using his ferocious intellect to fool, to protect Helen, to bury his childhood deep down dark. Back then he'd prayed every night that God would help him hide the truth, be a man, that he wouldn't be found out for what he was, a frightened little boy.

Get it together, Liam.

"I guess… I mean, I should get used to it because I'm going to be that way someday. Deaf." There, he'd said it. "And then it will all be over and done with."

"No," Maggie said. "You'll learn to hear in other ways, with people to help you."

Other ways…people to help you. How sure she was, how steady. But he was not. Inside he was stumbling still, the boy playing the man, little feet in grown-up shoes. It was too much.

"Yeah, well, that's a problem for another day, right?" He gently slid his hand from underneath hers. He felt her hurt. It was not fair what he'd just done, especially when he knew she'd stepped far out on a limb to prop him up the night before. Now, right now, she was offering him the chance to have something richer, a relationship that mattered, a soul-deep connection. He knew it, he craved it, yet the little boy in the man clothes was still terrified to have his vulnerability on display. So he turned the conversation to other things.

Maggie leaned away slightly, almost imperceptibly, and he was both relieved and grieved.

The miles passed with polite conversation until he noticed a car in his rearview mirror, far enough back but holding steady.

She picked up on his tension. "Someone behind us?"

"Maybe. White car, noticed it a mile or two back." Liam guided the truck over one lane. The white car stayed right with them. She heard Liam's sharp intake of breath as the car zoomed closer. With a spine-jarring jolt, it rammed their rear bumper.

Maggie was hurled forward against the tightening seat belt.

"Hold on," Liam said.

She clutched the door handle as he labored to keep the truck from skidding into the shoulder.

Her senses dizzied. He shot off the freeway onto an off-ramp. "Gonna try and lose him. Can you get a license number?"

Though she twisted in the seat and peered behind them, she could not make out the driver or the plates. "I think the front plate is obscured," she said.

They rolled into town and joined in a line of cars squeaking through a yellow light.

Maggie stared out the back window, heart thundering. "He's gone."

Liam exhaled. "Excellent. I'll pull in somewhere to call Danny."

She nodded, and he peeled off at a busy strip mall, engine idling. The minutes passed. No white car followed them in.

He relaxed, but not completely. "Guess we're clear. Let's wait a while, make sure he's not going to surprise us."

"I'm going to use the restroom. Then I'll wait in the coffee shop," she said, letting herself out of the truck. "Tell me when you want to leave."

He watched her for a moment, striding for the shop, jacket zipped up to her chin. It was her way of detaching from him, like he'd done to her. He deserved it.

I'm sorry, Maggie. Real sorry.

He had to wait on hold for a while to talk to Danny. When they hung up, he decided to go inside and fetch Maggie rather than text her. It was the least he could do. With a sigh, he heaved himself out of the truck, determined that he would still be a good-mannered cowboy, even if he was a coward.

SIXTEEN

Maggie was on the phone with Tammy when Liam entered the coffee shop. She stepped onto the porch to finish the call, dreading getting back into the truck with Liam.

She'd understood his earlier rebuff. He'd needed her the night before, but when morning came and his hearing had returned, he hadn't wanted her close, not in that way. How had she ever let herself imagine for one red second that there might be something possible between them? Maybe it was her sister's silly talk.

But Tammy had never managed to secure a relationship that didn't end in angst or downright disaster. So why on earth had she listened to her twin about Liam? She loved her sister with every atom of her being, but Tammy was not exactly qualified to dispense advice in the romance department, even if she had found a doting computer programmer.

Maggie finished assuring Tammy that they'd

seen no further sign of the white car that had rammed them and ended the call as Liam exited the shop. She followed him to the parking lot, determined at least to let herself into the truck before he did, but he stopped so suddenly she plowed into him. He didn't budge, but she stumbled back and he shot out an arm to keep her behind.

"Stay here."

She stayed put but watched closely as he did a quick walk around the truck and the nearby cars. He smacked his hat on his thigh and she saw what disturbed him. Two flat tires, the puncture marks showing clearly.

"He must have parked down the road and snuck in on foot, stayed low under cover of the other cars when I went in to get you." He looked at her. "Who knew we were headed to see Yoriko?"

She tried to recall. "Tammy and Joe. Whoever was around in the Lodge when we discussed it." Her stomach clenched and she bit her lip.

"What?"

"Virgil. At the parade. He was close by when I talked to Yoriko. He could have heard." She groaned. "I'm just real bad at the subterfuge thing."

He smiled at her. "I'd worry if you were real good at keeping secrets."

Not as good as you.

He pulled out his phone.

"Who are you calling?"

"Chad. We need some backup."

After the call Liam went to work on one flattened tire. By the time Chad arrived with a second spare tire, he had already finished changing the first.

Chad rolled out the tire. He opened his mouth to say something when Jingles exploded from the back seat, bounding over to Liam and yipping with excitement.

"What did you bring him for?" Liam demanded.

Chad looked sheepish. "He whined all day in the yard. After I took your call, he jumped the fence and climbed into my vehicle and wouldn't get out for anything. Dunno how he knew I was coming to meet you."

Liam's utter befuddlement made Maggie burst into an uncontrollable spurt of laughter. She was still wiping her eyes when Liam and Chad muscled on the second tire, Jingles sitting contentedly by her side, watching their every move.

Liam did not even try to redirect Jingles to Chad's vehicle when they loaded up again. "The dog is like a bad cold. You just can't shake him," Liam sighed. "It's ludicrous."

Maggie scratched Jingles behind the ears. "I guess since you've given him a candy cane, he's yours for life, Cowboy Santa."

Liam grimaced and rolled his eyes. They started out of the parking lot, Chad keeping pace behind them.

"Is he coming with us?" she asked.

"He's going to hang back, keep an eye on things."

Maggie considered that if Virgil had slashed the tires, he might be trying to slow them down to get ahead of them to Yoriko's shop. The clock was ticking for Virgil. If Tammy had left the jewelry with Yoriko, Virgil would do anything to stop them from retrieving it.

The lighthouse.

The parade.

The torched Corvette.

You don't want to be standing between a man and his goals. Accidents happen.

Virgil had already been able to get close, very close, and knowing he was out there now, waiting and watching, made her skin crawl.

"Maggie?"

She started, unaware that he'd been paying attention to her mood. "He's not gonna get what he wants. We're gonna win."

She wondered what that would look like. Winning meant Virgil wouldn't get his money but Tammy might very well go to jail. Or would it be better for Tammy if they didn't find it? But Bill would be victimized by a traitorous nephew and Virgil might continue to stalk them anyway.

The truth shall set you free, she thought.

She prayed that finding out the truth about the jewelry would somehow release them from Virgil's trap. Then Maggie would be ready to leave Driftwood, and Liam, far behind.

She watched him from the corner of her eye, broad-shouldered, determined, so strong and so vulnerable at the same time. What they could have had... What she imagined, for the sweetest of moments, they might have meant to each other...

Ignoring a pain in her chest, Maggie set her shoulders and stared straight ahead as Liam exited the freeway and the crashing Pacific came into view.

They pulled up at the address on Yoriko's business card, which turned out to be a minuscule shop sandwiched in between a rustic cluster of stores that faced a surf shop, a bicycle rental place and a cliff side with beach access.

The interior of her shop was cluttered with shelves full of colored glass items: ornaments, bowls, platters and a skinny Christmas tree sparkling with blown glass icicles. There was hardly enough room for three of them, so Chad waited on the doorstep with his hands in his pockets.

"He told me his dad taught him to pocket his hands whenever they went into a store," Liam whispered to Maggie.

She smiled. "Sounds like a smart dad. I'd like to meet him someday."

Liam's grin flickered. "Chad's got a difficult story. Not my place to tell it. He's doing great things. Trying to start a therapy program for veterans and horses on the ranch. Good man."

She caught Chad's silent profile as he scanned the parking lot. He had his own troubled path, it seemed, and it didn't surprise her. Still waters could run very deep indeed.

Maggie rang the tiny bell on the counter. There wasn't much of a back room, just a tacked-up curtain separating the office area from the front. Liam had circled around the counter, reaching to grasp the curtain, when a young woman walked through, startled.

Liam apologized. "We're looking for Yoriko."

She flipped her blond ponytail behind her shoulder and Maggie thought something wary crept into her eyes. "You, too?"

"Too?" Maggie's eyes rounded. "Someone else was here looking for her?"

"A guy called. Said he wanted to talk to her,

but like I told him, she isn't here. She asked me to look over the shop for a little while. I work at the bike rental place. Do you want to buy something? I can ring you up."

"We need to speak to Yoriko," Maggie said. "She's a friend of my sister's. She asked us to come."

Again the woman's eyes looked over Liam and Maggie and then her gaze drifted to Chad, lingering on him for a moment, then moving back to Maggie. "You look familiar."

"I haven't been here before but you might have seen my sister, Tammy. We're twins. Like I said, she and Yoriko are friends."

That got a smile of recognition. "Oh yeah. Your sister used to help Yoriko out and once in a while she'd rent a bike. That's why I know your face, or hers anyway."

Maggie returned the smile. "We really need to talk to Yoriko. Will she be back soon?"

"I hope so, but there's, uh, been some trouble."

Tension zinged through Maggie's nerves. "What kind of trouble?"

"I guess it's okay to tell you. Yoriko had a bunch of her merch—you know, her Christmas stock—loaded up in a van to deliver to the Lodge for the festival on Wednesday. It was parked out back and someone broke into it early this morning."

Liam blew out a breath. "Damage?"

"Some. Mostly the boxes were thrown around."

Thrown around, as if someone was searching. Maggie knew Liam was thinking the same thing.

The woman glanced at Chad as he knelt to scratch the ears of an old tabby cat that had crept close. "I helped her clean up the mess and she pulled some inventory from the back to replace the broken stuff. That's where she is now. She left me a note on the door that she'd driven to her house to pick up some other items but she'd be back as soon as she could. She lives on the bluff at Sea Cliff. The only house there. Sorry, but I don't have her cell number."

"Did you tell the man on the phone where Yoriko lives?" Liam said.

"Nah. I'm only telling you because I know Yoriko really loves Tammy. I'm not sure exactly when she left, so I don't know when she'll return. You can wait if you want."

Her gaze drifted appreciatively to Chad on the porch. He noticed her attention and gave her a polite nod. "He can come in, too."

Maggie squelched a smile. The allure of a handsome dark-eyed cowboy was working. She'd not noticed that Chad had a girlfriend in the time she'd been on the ranch, but it seemed this young lady was eager to remedy that problem.

An older couple crowded into the shop and Liam and Maggie squeezed out to give them room.

"Gonna have to split up," Liam said after he filled Chad in, "so we don't miss her."

Chad nodded. "Okay. I'll stay here if you two want to go to her house."

"All right," Liam agreed. "But Virgil didn't find what he was looking for the first time. He rammed us and flattened my tires to slow us down so he could track Yoriko. If he didn't find out her address, could be he comes back here to look again, only he's running out of time. Watch yourself."

Chad nodded.

"Oh," Liam said with a sly grin. "Seems like the lady inside is an admirer of your movie star good looks."

Chad's cheeks went ruddy and he looked at his boots. "Oh, knock it off."

"Just thought you should know which way the wind is blowing, brother," Liam quipped as they made their way to his truck.

Chad mumbled some sort of a reply, which did not sound complimentary, but Maggie noticed him dart a quick look from under his hat toward the young lady in the shop.

Liam's playful mood dissipated as they pulled back onto the road. "Wish we had gotten a cell number for Yoriko. Could have warned her about Virgil."

"You think he'll head for her house? How would he know where to find it?"

"Same way we know. People here are friendly. They talk."

She lives on the bluff at Sea Cliff. The only house there.

He pressed the accelerator until the truck was taking the turns at the maximum speed limit. To the west stretched green grassy fields dotted with cattle. To the right, black cliffs seemed to reach out to the darkening sky as the day headed toward sunset. And ahead? She prayed they would not find any more evidence of Virgil's ruthless desire to reclaim what Tammy had taken.

SEVENTEEN

Liam parked next to the van in the narrow driveway. Yoriko's was a more modern house than he'd pictured, a tidy two-story with a composite roof and wide glass windows that faced the sea. Liam figured it would be nice to have a panorama of the ocean, but he'd miss seeing the fields change color from green to the rich gold brown in the dry summer months. No doubt about it, he was a land creature through and through. He saw no sign of any other vehicles, but there were plenty of wooded and rocky places nearby where Virgil could conceal his car if he had found his way there ahead of them.

"Why don't you—" he started but Maggie was already out of the truck and approaching the front door. He rolled down the window halfway for Jingles and told him to stay. It was more wishful thinking than a command, he knew.

As he got out, Jingles fired him a peevish look and plopped down on the seat. Liam goggled when he saw the candy cane tucked under Jingles's crooked paw. It was covered with lint and dust. "Aren't you gonna eat that thing after all the trouble?"

Jingles shot out his tongue to swipe at the cane and then laid his head on his paws with a plaintive sigh.

"There is something seriously weird about that dog," he grumbled, catching up to Maggie just as the front door opened a crack. Yoriko peeped out, eyes framed by a fringe of dark bangs threaded with silver.

"I'm Maggie Lofton," Maggie said. "You gave me your card at the parade."

The woman's round face relaxed.

After a moment, he heard the chain pull back and she opened the door. "Oh yes. Of course."

Maggie introduced Liam. "May we have a few minutes of your time?"

She opened the door and ushered them into a room minimally furnished with expensive pieces, not one of which, to Liam, looked nearly as comfortable as the ragged old couch at the bunkhouse. On the wall above a gas fireplace hung a lovely watercolor of the ocean, which he admired before sending a quick text to Chad to tell him they'd found Yoriko at home.

She gestured them into a leather-covered love

seat and took the richly upholstered chair opposite them.

"I'm afraid my sister got into some trouble," Maggie said. "And I think the person she angered may have been the one who broke into your van. We think he rammed us and slashed our tires to prevent us from getting here to talk to you."

Yoriko listened intently as Maggie described the situation. She told Yoriko everything, including her sister's impromptu theft.

Liam was relieved when Yoriko smiled. "Yes, that sounds like Tammy. She is not one to deliberate before she acts, but she does have a heart of gold. She helped in my shop many times and wouldn't take any payment. She said it was reward enough to be near the beach."

"You indicated she left something here?" Maggie said.

Yoriko opened a drawer and handed Maggie a pink knit cap.

Maggie stared. "This is it? This is what you meant?"

Yoriko slowly nodded her head and he saw Maggie's shoulders droop along with his own. He wanted to reach out to her.

"But I thought…" Maggie started.

Yoriko looked confused. "She was upset when she arrived here by cab Wednesday afternoon, exhausted. I thought at first she might be sick. She was near tears but she did not want to discuss the reason. I made her lie down and prepared some tea. It didn't help her agitation, so I wasn't surprised when she said she wanted to walk on the beach to clear her mind."

"Okay," Maggie said. "And after that? Did she say where she'd been or might be headed?"

"To Driftwood, I think."

"Probably to meet with Danny Patron," Maggie said to Liam.

"She looked sick. I couldn't convince her to stay. She wanted to call her boyfriend, but she didn't have her phone and she couldn't remember the number, and that upset her deeply."

"So she stayed with you for a few hours, walked on the beach, then left for Driftwood in another cab?" Liam asked.

Yoriko nodded.

He went on with his theorizing. "While she was in town, she couldn't get hold of Danny Patron." He looked at Maggie. "And then she showed up at the Lodge later that night."

"Where Helen took her in," Maggie said. "So we know where she was, mostly, but not where she left the jewelry. There's a gap in the timeline." She sighed, and Liam noticed smudges of fatigue shadowing her eyes. The whole situation had taken a terrible toll on both sisters.

"I thought..." she started. "I mean, I hoped she'd left the jewelry with you. I don't know where else to look."

Liam took her hand. "We'll figure something out."

Maggie grimaced. "Christmas Eve is Friday. The insurance company will make their decision. He'll get away with it."

"No," he said with more conviction than the facts warranted. "He won't."

Yoriko interrupted. "Wait a minute. I just remembered something...the backpack."

Maggie jerked. "What backpack?"

Yoriko was thoughtful for a moment. "When she arrived, she had a backpack, a pink one. She held on to it as if it was a baby."

"Did she take it with her when she left your house?"

"That's the funny thing. I didn't think of it until just now, but she had the backpack when she went for her beach walk." Yoriko leaned forward. "And when she came back, she didn't."

Maggie gripped Liam's hand and he squeezed back, sharing in her rush of hope.

"Maggie," he said, "do you think it's possible Tammy hid the jewelry on the beach somewhere?"

"I absolutely do," she said, still clutching his fingers tight.

He tried to be practical. "It's almost dark. We should come back tomorrow, or at least wait for Chad to get here."

Maggie shook her head. "We have to look." She got up, a question in her expression, those autumn eyes pleading as she searched his face. "I know it's not optimal, but please, will you go with me now?"

Caught in that gaze, powerless against her determination to save her sister at all costs, he knew he would go here, there, anywhere in the world she asked him. That thought set him back a pace as he revisited the fear he'd experienced that coiled him up inside and remained lying in wait. He didn't deserve her, couldn't be enough for her, but she drew him like a horse heading for the barn and he couldn't help himself. He cleared his throat. "Sure, yes. We'd better get a move on. Sundown in less than an hour. I have flashlights in my truck."

"And a canine lookout," Maggie added.

He grimaced. "Oh, man. Do we have to take Jingles?"

"Yes," she said firmly.

Liam nodded.

They thanked Yoriko as she escorted them outside.

"If you walk to the steps, there's a trail that cuts along the cliff face and down to the shore.

It's slippery and the tide's coming in soon, so you'll have to move quickly."

Liam tipped his hat. "Thank you, ma'am."

"I hope you find what you're looking for."

"Me, too," he said, releasing the exuberant dog from the back seat of his truck and grabbing the flashlights. He sent another text to Chad and hurried after Maggie, matching her stride for determined stride.

The wind barreling off the ocean bit at Maggie, but she hardly noticed it. She well knew Tammy's penchant for the dramatic. They'd spent a whole summer staying at their grandparents' lakeside cabin when they were children, burying treasure boxes and digging them up. If there was a pirate adventure they'd not acted out, she didn't know what it would be. Tammy would not hesitate to hide the jewelry in some isolated place—the more theatrical, the better. If she thought Virgil was closing in, the beach might be the perfect spot.

"Yoriko says this is a private beach access, so if Tammy did hide something, we can hope it hasn't been found by a wandering beachcomber," she called over her shoulder. The cliff trail became steeper as they descended, merely a groove cut into the rugged black rock.

His boots slipped now and again, but Maggie

moved easily as the trail plunged downward. Jingles was his usual oblivious self, stopping to lick or sniff periodically as they made their way along. At least he'd left his candy cane in the truck.

The pounding waves made Liam's good ear vibrate and his unease grew. It was entirely possible that Virgil had taken up position and was tracking them at that very moment. Chad was on his way, probably only another fifteen minutes from their location. He'd told Yoriko about Chad so as not to startle her with yet another stranger arriving on her property. They had easily another fifty minutes before the sun would sink below the horizon and they were nearing surf level. Plenty of time.

They emerged onto a flat crescent of pebbled sand. Haphazard piles of boulders lay here and there, creating a sandy labyrinth. Jingles set off to sniff each pockmarked rock, while he and Maggie searched.

"It would have to be up higher," he mused, "or the water would get it. There's…"

"I see it," Maggie called.

She pointed to the gaping mouth of a cave some fifteen feet above them, a dark maw gouged into the side of the cliff. They had not seen it in their descent but Tammy would have. Maybe she'd even explored it previously.

"How do we get up there?" he mused.

Maggie found it before he did, the little trail of handholds that led seemingly straight up. "Great," he said, noting that his boot tops were now submerged by the intruding tide.

She started up first, using her hands to pull herself along. He did the same. Jingles watched from below, barking in encouragement or dismay, Liam could not tell which.

He was good and winded by the time they reached the cave. Scrambling inside, he could not stand comfortably in the six-foot-high space. There was not much room to turn around, either, because of the rock projections that poked from every direction.

Maggie made it farther in, peering into the dark corners with the aid of his flashlight. "It has to be here," she said.

"Possible someone found it?" Someone, like Virgil? Had he beaten them to the treasure?

"No," she snapped. "Not possible."

So he held his tongue and crept around as best he could, banging his forehead and knee in the process. The place was suited for wiry wilderness guides, not cowboys. After a solid ten minutes, he checked below. "We've got to scoot. Tide's coming in."

"I know it's here, it has to be." She said something else. He didn't get the words but he deciphered the tone. He circled her wrist with his fingers.

"We can come back tomorrow, but it's getting unsafe here now. I think Jingles is practicing his doggy paddling."

She tensed against his touch, determination warring with her good sense. Finally she sighed and allowed him to lead her to the opening. She turned once more, as if to say goodbye to the rocky nest. He felt her stiffen.

"There." She pointed.

"Where?"

He didn't hear Maggie's answer, or maybe she didn't give one. Instead she scrambled up onto a pinnacle of damp rock and snatched something from behind it. "I saw a tiny bit of pink," she said, triumphantly, holding the backpack up for him to see.

He couldn't restrain himself from wrapping her and the pink backpack in a bear hug and lifting her off the ground, inviting himself to join in her excitement and joy. In that little corner of the frigid cave, he felt suddenly warm.

When he put her down, she unzipped the pack, her excitement palpable. "There's a long black box in here. Dark, like velvet."

Jingles's anxious yip from below carried over the waves. "Let's take it back and look. Gonna lose the light soon."

She followed him out, sliding the pink pack straps over her shoulders.

The journey down took longer than it had going up and the seawater was knee level when he reached the shore, where Jingles was standing on a flat rock to avoid the rising water.

They started immediately back up the cliff trail. Liam tried to keep his mind from wandering as they climbed higher and higher. They'd actually done it, found the jewelry Tammy had hidden. It bordered on the incredible that their investigation had paid off. Things were finally starting to look up. Danny Patron would help them find a legal way out for Tammy, he was certain. Best of all, they'd thwarted Virgil's plans to rip off his uncle.

Ahead, the cliff trail pinched off and forced them out onto an exposed area of rock that projected over the deep water. The frigid cold blasted them without mercy. Jingles's nails did not provide enough purchase and he slipped and skidded until Liam scooped him up, earning himself a sloppy tongue bath.

"Don't get excited, dog," he grumbled. "I—" The words were snatched away as Maggie rounded the turn ahead of him. Something, he could not tell if it was a bat or a branch, swept out of the darkness and knocked her over.

Hands scrambled and tore at her backpack.

Liam released Jingles and grabbed for Maggie at the same time, trying to pull her to him. Someone else was reaching for her, face lost in the gloom, fumbling for the backpack. He shot out a fist and drove the guy back, but not before the attacker grabbed a backpack strap and straight-armed Maggie. Liam saw her eyes go round with shock, her fear caught by the moonlight as she plummeted backward into the ocean below. Liam did not hesitate as he dived into the water after her.

EIGHTEEN

Maggie flailed in a futile attempt to save herself as she fell. She hit the water hard, the impact driving the air from her lungs. Reflexively she gulped to refill them, sucking in icy salt water. Cold swamped her senses. When she broke the surface again, a wave crashed over her head, spinning her around to confront the black rocks that appeared and disappeared behind fountaining water.

Her brain struggled to process what had happened. She'd been grabbed at by someone waiting on the trail and his shove had sent her into the ocean. Did she still have the backpack on? She couldn't feel anything but the biting cold and fear as the waves forced her closer to the jagged rocks.

"Liam," she tried to shout. Was he still on the trail? Could he hear her screams? A wall of water lifted her up and slammed her back down again. A submerged rock cut into her knee and the ocean swallowed her cry of pain.

A movement to her right sent her churning backward, praying it was not a shark attracted by her thrashing. "Liam," she tried to scream again, only to be deluged by another mountain of water. Something brushed her leg. Terror galvanized her into frantic swimming, which did nothing against the power of the ocean. It was harder to keep her chin above the water now as cold began to leach the strength from her muscles, numbing her an inch at a time.

She struck out again, trying to swim parallel to the jagged rocks, seeking a more hospitable patch of coast to aim for, but the waves tossed and tumbled her too violently. She seemed to be moving in circles.

A snout broke the water near her elbow. Her scream died away as she recognized the matted wet fur. "Jingles," she cried.

He barked, and Liam swam up behind him.

"Liam, here!" She gulped a mouthful of foam.

He didn't answer as he fought his way over and held her to him, her head tucked under his chin for a moment, his breathing erratic.

"Gonna try to get us a little north of here. Saw a spot of sand. Hold on to me."

She asked him to make sure the backpack was still zipped securely, but he did not appear to hear her. The ocean water had probably ruined his hearing aid. Even without her direction, he reached for the backpack and secured it to his shoulders. "Come on, Jingles."

The dog paddled along next to them. Maggie gave it all her effort, but she was so cold, so battered by the surf, she could not make any progress. The ocean was like a claw, pinching her.

Liam looped an arm around her and towed her next to him. At one point, he was washed off balance. The waves tossed them both over, slamming them into a flat shelf of rock. Liam grunted as he pushed mightily to get them away from the sharp ledge. She kicked and thrashed as well, grabbing Jingles and holding him close, fearful that he was not strong enough to keep from being battered to pieces. Jingles continued to paddle his legs as if she had not interrupted his efforts. Stroke by painful stroke, they pulled closer to the shore until she felt the sliding sand under her shoes.

Half laughing, half crying, she collapsed on the shore with Jingles next to her, limbs in spasm with cold and effort. She wanted nothing more than to lie there and experience the sheer joy of breathing in and out on solid ground. Liam was lifting her, carrying her farther away from the waves into the shadow of a boulder pile.

He squeezed her so tight to his chest that she

almost couldn't get a breath. "I couldn't... I mean... I..." He stopped talking, bent his head to hers and kissed her.

His mouth was cold, but the connection sent a spark through her that revived her spirit. She wound her arms around his neck. It was so right to have him close, so perfect, that for a moment she forgot the chaos of their situation and surrendered herself to the kiss, thanking God they had not drowned.

He eased back and looked down at her, his expression impossible to decipher. Relieved? Tender? Hopeful? After a beat more, he jerked back a pace to listen.

"What is it?" she asked, but of course he didn't hear. He patted his pockets and pulled out a sodden phone. His expression told her it was beyond hope. She reached out a shivering hand and turned his face to hers. "What?"

He was shivering, too, water snaking down from his hair along his strong jaw. "Not sure where he is."

"Who? Virgil?"

Liam didn't answer. He looked at Jingles and she realized he was watching to see if Jingles was picking up the sound of someone approaching. Jingles appeared calm, if trembling with cold. He gave a mighty shake and sprayed them both with water.

A long, piercing whistle cracked through the night. Jingles barked.

Liam shot her a questioning look. She mimed a whistle and pointed to the cliff top.

She saw his shoulders relax. "Chad. He's here. He'll look out for us."

Liam put two fingers to his mouth and returned a whistle of his own.

"If he heard me, he'll come help," Liam said. "But if my brain's not too addled, Yoriko's house is right up there on the bluff. Do you think you can make it?"

She nodded and he took her hand. She struggled to her feet, leaning on him more than she wanted.

He frowned. "Hurt?"

"I banged my knee on a rock."

He leaned close and put two fingers to her lips. "Say it again."

My knee, she mouthed as his fingertip grazed her lips, reading the message through his touch.

She held on to his shoulders while he bent and examined her knee. Before she realized what was happening, he scooped her up into his arms.

"I can walk," she protested.

Whether he heard her this time or not, he didn't acknowledge, and merely started off along the sand, Jingles following.

* * *

Chad met them halfway. Liam placed Maggie between them and they helped her to Yoriko's house. His insides were still a twisted mess at how close he'd come to losing Maggie, but one boot in front of the other was all that was required of him at the moment.

Yoriko bustled around, lighting the fireplace and spiriting Maggie away into the bedroom.

Chad produced a sweatshirt from the truck so at least Liam's torso was dry. He also procured an extra hearing aid Liam kept in the glove box, and a towel that Liam used to dry Jingles.

Liam sat on the stone fireplace hearth with Jingles curled around his shins and let the blessed warmth seep in. His body still trembled, partly from the cold. He worked hard to keep out the feelings about what he'd just experienced. The kiss they'd shared was his way of saying what he dared not. Adrift in that monstrous ocean with no way to hear her cries...

"Danny's working a traffic accident, but he'll call ASAP and dispatch an officer," Chad said, interrupting his thoughts. "Yoriko told me where you'd gone, and I went looking for you. I saw someone fall into the water. Wasn't close enough to know it was Maggie."

"Did you see anyone else?"

"I saw you dive into the water and someone running away toward the road."

"Why didn't you stop him?"

Chad frowned. "Seemed to me a better choice to call for help and try to get close enough to help you and Maggie."

Liam blew out a breath. "Yeah. It was. Sorry."

Chad lifted a shoulder and Liam caught the mischievous smile. "You had things handled, I guess. Besides, you looked real sharp in your pink backpack."

Liam fired him a look and could not resist a grin that turned into a chuckle. "Takes a real manly cowboy to pull off a pink backpack." He was dying to open the backpack to see the jewels that had almost resulted in them both being drowned. But it was one of his guiding principles in life, taught to him by his sister, that a man should never, ever, pry inside a woman's purse. He figured the rule probably applied to backpacks, too, especially pink ones.

Maggie limped out from the bedroom and he sprang to his feet to help her settle next to him on the hearth. She was wearing a borrowed sweat suit that was a couple inches too short in every direction. Her left pant leg was bunched up, revealing a neat bandage on her knee. Jingles licked her exposed calf as she sat. Her lips were still a bluish color, but she was not shivering quite as much. Still he made sure she was directly in line to receive maximum warmth from the fire.

"I cleaned out the wound and disinfected it," Yoriko said. "It's not deep, but there's going to be quite a nasty bruise."

"We'll go to the hospital as soon as—" he started.

"No, we won't," Maggie said, "unless you need to be seen."

"No, ma'am," he said. "Me and the dog are fine."

Her eyes went to the backpack. "I can't believe we finally got it."

A phone ringing made her jump. Chad answered and clicked on the speaker. "Trying to get an officer there," Danny said, "but we've got a real mess of an accident here so I'm still on the scene. Do you need an ambulance?"

"No," Liam said. "We're okay, just cold."

"Hiking at night on the beach is not advisable," Danny joked after a beat or two.

"Yeah," Liam retorted. "We figured that out."

Danny listened while Liam and Maggie each gave their statements.

"You were followed from the glass shop, clearly," Danny said. "Someone is doing a pretty efficient job menacing you two, not to mention almost causing a wreck and flattening your tires."

"Not someone. It was Virgil. He's the one with everything to lose," Liam growled.

In the background they heard Danny speak to someone on his radio before he returned to the phone. "Seems you're right about his level of desperation. He's in debt up to his eyeballs. He needs that insurance claim to go through so he can help himself to more of Uncle Bill's money. The jewelry policy was worth $100,000, so that's a hefty motive."

Maggie hugged herself. "Did you contact his granddaughter?"

"Yes, and she has nothing good to say about Virgil. She's making arrangements to come back to the States, but she has three kids, so that may take a while. In the meantime, I visited personally with Bill. He has periods of clarity and some uncertain spells. All in all, he seems capable of making his own decisions and unwilling to believe his nephew is milking him."

Danny again spoke to someone and then returned to their conversation. "Virgil's showed him the video and convinced him that Tammy is at fault for the theft. Further, Bill's been persuaded that she's the one who's been stealing from him, which necessitated him taking out the policy on the jewelry in the first place."

"He's being brainwashed," Maggie snapped. "That's elder abuse."

"I've asked one of my officers to dig deeper into that, but for now there's no hard evidence that Virgil's committed a crime."

"Tammy heard him arranging to have the necklace stolen," Maggie reminded him. "That's a crime."

Danny sighed. "Hearing and proving…" His voice was drowned out for a moment by engine noise. "And I suppose when I ask questions, Virgil is going to have an airtight alibi for his whereabouts during your ocean escapade just now."

A slow burn began in Liam's gut. "No doubt."

"Fine," Maggie said, snatching up the backpack. "At least he's not going to get his hands on the insurance money." She unzipped the backpack and pulled out the long velvet box. It was secured with a sturdy rubber band.

She laid it on her lap and removed the band. Liam thought he saw tears gathering in her eyes. "And Bill will have his wife's jewelry back. That's something, right?"

He nodded. It would not provide much comfort if Tammy was jailed for the theft, but he knew Maggie was hanging on by a thread, looking for some silver lining that would mean

Virgil wouldn't emerge unscathed after almost killing them.

She opened the box. The lid fell to the floor. In the perfect stillness of the moment, tears rolled down her face and her shocked gasp rang clear as anything in his ears.

NINETEEN

Maggie upended the box and took out the lining. It was empty. She unzipped all the backpack pockets and turned the whole thing upside down, shaking it with no result. The jewelry was nowhere to be found.

"Did someone take it?" she managed to ask. "Some beach visitor?"

Danny was still listening in. "Unlikely they would have found it, and more unlikely they would have taken the jewelry, refastened the rubber band and hidden the backpack again."

"Virgil?" she rasped.

Liam shook his head. "But then why bother to steal it now? It couldn't have been him."

Maggie exhaled. "Tammy must have left the box as a ruse. She was afraid Virgil was following her. She hid the backpack as a diversion in case he followed her."

"Any chance she's remembered where she took it after that?" Danny asked.

Maggie groaned, trying to keep from wailing outright. "As of this morning, she didn't even remember coming to Yoriko's in the first place. I'll ask her, but I'm sure she would have told me if she recalled anything."

Liam ended the call with Danny, wiped a hand across his damp forehead. "You can call her from the ranch, since our phones are ruined."

"She's going to be devastated," Maggie said, hardly able to force the words out. Her body was battered and her spirit, too. She'd been so hopeful that they could put an end to Virgil's threats with a visit to Yoriko. The sense of defeat left her dull and slow, so she let Liam lead her to the truck and help her inside. Jingles was exhausted, too, and quickly took his spot in the back seat.

They rode in silence, thoughts bumping untidily through her brain. What was the next move? Was there even going to be another opportunity to find the jewels before the deadline? She had not one single idea of where else to look. Liam was unusually still, his mouth pinched with some thoughts he did not share. The miles seemed endless as they made their way back to the ranch.

Wearily she allowed him to lead her into the

saddlery. He took off his hat and stared at her for a moment.

"What?"

He looked away. "Nothing."

Impatience bubbled up through the stress. "Not nothing. Something. You tried to tell me on the beach. What?"

He quickly covered the uncertain look with a grin. "No, really. Just glad you're okay. That was some swimming pool we climbed out of."

"Liam," she said, plopping the backpack on the floor, "why don't you quit hiding behind that jolly cowboy demeanor and tell me what you think?"

He blinked, mouth pinched. "I'm not hiding."

"Yes, you are."

She saw him jerk and she knew she was being harsh, but the evening, the kiss, the disappointment and the relief all jumbled inside and stripped away her self-control. This man, this cowboy, had invaded her every thought and dream and it was time to clear the air between them. "You don't want to talk about things like feelings and worries and fears, so you spit out a joke or a witticism because you're scared, like you were scared when you lost your hearing after the car fire."

He stepped back, palms up. "You've had a bad night, we both have. It's not the right time…"

"Yes, it is," she cried. "It's the perfect time, Liam. Tell me what's going on in here." She poked a finger at his chest. The contact seemed to spark his anger.

"All right," he snapped. "You want to know? I was scared out of my mind tonight. You wanna know why exactly? You want me to share that?"

She nodded.

Tension sizzled in the stark lines bracketing his mouth. "Because I couldn't hear you calling for help in that ocean, Maggie. I could not make out where you were and all I could think of was that you were gonna drown." Desperation crackled through the words.

"Liam…" she whispered, anger slipping away.

"Know how I found you?" His jaw was tight, lips pinched. "You want to know how the big, tough cowboy found you? Jingles. He heard you screaming and made a beeline for you and I followed. So that's it, Maggie. Is that what you wanted to hear me say? You would have been dead if it weren't for my dog?"

"Listen to me," she said, harder than she meant. "I don't think any less of you because of your hearing loss. You're still the same man."

"Oh yeah?" He pulled the hearing aid from his ear. His face was stark with emotion. "How about now? How about if you're screaming for help or maybe I'm on the tractor and little Charlie's right behind and I don't hear him? Huh? You won't think any less of me then?"

"No," she said, chin up so he could hear. "No."

He jammed the aid back in his ear and spun around to go. "Well, I would."

She grabbed his shirtsleeve, stopping him. "And that's the problem, Liam. You've been showing the world you're in charge since you were a boy. You've tended your sister, a household, all the adult decisions by yourself, but you don't have to anymore. That's not what God wants." She gripped his shirt tighter, trying to draw him closer past the anger and pain that separated them. "He made us to do things together..." She paused and gulped. "You and me."

Liam's eyes blazed with myriad emotions she could not sort out as he looked down at her, his broad shoulders gradually slumping. "Maggie... when you're near me, I almost believe that."

Her heart swelled. She could not deny that she cared about Liam in a way that made her want more. She tipped her face to his, certain that he must see it, too, the emotion that filled her. *Liam, let me in.*

"You deserve someone to take care of you," he murmured, tracing a finger down her cheek. "And someone to hear every word you ever say."

He clutched her to him then and buried his face in her hair, and she held her breath.

"It doesn't matter," she murmured, "as long as I have you."

His breath hitched, she heard it, and then he sighed, soft and low. "Don't care for me, Maggie," he whispered. "You deserve better."

"Liam…" she started, but he broke from their embrace and left, the door banging sharply behind him.

For a moment she stood paralyzed, as if she was still lost in the ocean. What had just passed between them had the tone of finality to it. Pain surged hot and sharp. She wandered in helpless circles, uncertain about what to do. Finally she called her sister, but her phone went unanswered.

How could Tammy help anyway? And she'd have to share the outcome of their beach adventure. The anguish could wait until tomorrow morning. Maggie had a heart full enough for one night.

She lay on the small bed and tried to sleep, tossing and turning with memories of the awful night, the horrible grip of the waves, the devastating disappointment of not saving her sister and the anguish of her conversation with Liam.

It was no wonder the hands of the clock ticked

away the time until forty-five minutes later a rap sounded on the door.

Liam, she thought, her breath quickening. She flung open the door, breath caught in surprise.

"Joe? What's wrong? Is it Tammy?"

His pallor was ghastly in the pale moonlight. She drew him in and turned on the lamp. "What happened?"

"He's got her."

"What?"

"Virgil. He's taken Tammy. He called from her phone and told me he'd been trying to get you, but your phone was disconnected."

"Ruined from the water," she said mechanically, her nerves firing to life. "What...what did he say in the message?"

"He said you'd recovered the jewelry and he wants it back. You're to bring it to Tammy's trailer right now, no police or cowboys. If not..."

"If not?" she prompted, terrified to hear the rest.

"He'll kill her."

Liam couldn't sleep. In the wee hours of Wednesday morning before the sun was up, he found himself hollow-eyed, unshaved, staring at the coffeepot in the bunkhouse, watching it drip. He wanted to go to the saddlery, to lose himself in the pieces waiting for his attention. The place always comforted him; the supple strength of the leather held such potential. Soft and strong, like a certain woman who'd arrowed right into his core. Maggie was there in the saddlery, for how much longer, he didn't know. They'd reached a dead end in their search for the jewelry. *A dead end for other things, too.*

You and me... She'd said that, revealed the feelings she had for him, and part of him was elated that she cared for him, wanted him, in spite of his weakness.

But Maggie didn't deserve a man who wore a mask, a man whose world was narrowing day by day. He felt anew the terror at not being able to find her in the waves.

A man who was flat-out scared.

What would happen in the future when he went completely deaf? He'd had to leave his beloved Green Berets. Would he have to let go of working the ranch, also? How would he make a living? Tend to a family?

Family. That notion amped up his nerves. Gus and Ginny had made him part of their brood and out of that he'd become uncle to a boy he adored. How would he hear the cheers from the Little League field when Charlie hit that homer? Listen to Charlie say his prayers at night? Hear the boy say, "I wuv you, Uncle Weeum."

Anger took hold of him and he slammed a

hand on the countertop. He'd never been one to feel like a victim. Hadn't he managed his family drama without complaint? Learned to let go of his military life? Why did God have to take away his chance with Maggie?

He made us to do things together.

But surely God wasn't trying to teach him that now, at this point in his life, when he'd made Liam to be a man to take care of others since he was seven years old?

"God," he said savagely, "what are you trying to do here? 'Cause I don't get it."

He was not surprised when he heard paws scratching on the front door. The dog had some uncanny way of knowing where and when to find Liam.

Sure enough, Jingles sat on the porch, gaze bright in the predawn gloom. Resigned, Liam let him in and poured kibble into a bowl. Jingles set about chomping it down in record time. Then he swiped a tongue over his mouth, sat back and regarded Liam with those unblinking eyes.

"I guess you aren't such a bad dog," Liam said, sinking to one knee and rubbing his ears. The dog turned to rubber, sliding on his back and presenting his tummy for Liam to scratch. He laughed. "Maybe you just aren't cut out for herding. But, hey, I never learned to cook, so I guess we can't be good at everything, right?"

Jingles's paws scrabbled in an invitation for Liam to keep up the tummy scratches. He thought about how this odd lump of a misfit animal had guided him through the waves to Maggie. "Yeah, you're a good dog, Jingles," he whispered. "A real good dog."

Jingles wriggled as Liam got to his feet. He still felt like a wrung-out towel, knowing how badly he'd let Maggie down, but something about the wacky dog's devotion encouraged him. When Jingles cocked an ear, Liam stepped outside to scan. A car he didn't recognize was just pulling out of the front gate, two figures in the front seat. It took him an extra minute to identify Joe as the driver and, in the passenger seat, Maggie.

"Where do you figure they're headed at this hour?"

Jingles was right on his heels as Liam shrugged on his barn jacket and headed to the truck.

TWENTY

Maggie clutched the pink backpack, trying to keep breathing through the panic. "How did he get to her?"

"I don't know." Joe's knuckles were white on the wheel. "This whole thing is crazy. We gotta just give him what he wants and get Tammy back safe. Did you have any success at Yoriko's?"

"We found something."

He looked at her strangely. "What do you mean? I thought for sure you'd find the jewelry."

"I'll explain later," she said, not wanting to bother with an explanation of the empty jewelry case. Goose bumps prickled her skin. What would Virgil do when he found out the case was empty? In the suspense movies Tammy loved to watch, the hero would have some clever plan, a diversion, a hidden backup guy. Maggie had nothing but one slender fragment of an idea: hand the backpack over, grab Tammy and run.

She wanted to explain to Joe that she had no idea where to look next for the ransom for her sister's life, but Joe's hands were already shaking, his Adam's apple bobbing up and down convulsively.

"Joe," she instructed as they headed up the graveled driveway to the trailer, "keep the engine running. Be ready to get us out of here quick."

He shot her a questioning look but there wasn't time for a follow-up as the light went on in Tammy's trailer.

Maggie got out of the car on rubbery legs.

Virgil stepped onto the porch. "Thanks for coming," he said as if they'd agreed to meet for lunch. "We'll all be glad when this situation is resolved."

"Where's my sister?" Maggie demanded.

Joe stood next to her. "Let us see her."

Virgil laughed. "You don't watch enough TV, do you? That's not how it works. Give me the jewelry."

"Not until I see that my sister is safe."

"Look," Virgil said, teeth bared, "I don't have time for this. I have people I owe and an insurance claim pending. Now I hear that Vivian is making arrangements to return to live with dear old Uncle Bill. I have you to thank for that."

Her mouth managed to form words in spite

of her bone-deep fear. "No, you have yourself to blame, trying to terrorize us, blackmailing my sister."

Hatred blazed in his eyes. "You're going to give me what I want. I'll settle things here with the insurance claim before dear Viv rolls into town."

"You've gone too far with this abduction," Joe said. "You crossed the line."

Virgil chuckled. "But I hold all the cards. I have Tammy. If you give me the jewelry, I'll let her go unharmed and erase the video of her theft." He snapped his fingers. "All this trouble goes away, just like that. Think of it as my Christmas present to you." He laughed. "A get-out-of-jail-free card. It's so much nicer than the alternative in which both women die."

Joe's teeth crunched together. "You were wrong to involve Tammy in all of this."

Virgil regarded him, chin cocked. "You have it bad for that girl, don't you?"

A branch cracked from behind them in the woods. Virgil flinched. He pulled a handgun from his belt and swiveled a glare at Maggie. "If you brought help, I'll shoot you right here, right now."

Her mouth went dry with terror. "I didn't tell anybody. I promise."

He wiggled his fingers at her. "Backpack. Now."

She forced her limbs into action, holding the backpack out to him.

"My sister..." she started.

He unzipped the backpack, darting looks at the woods behind him. He tossed out the jacket from the pack and grabbed the velvet box, the gun still secure in one hand.

"I want to see my sister," she cried, taking two steps toward the porch step.

But he'd stripped the rubber band off the box and flung it open. He howled at the sight of the empty box, aiming the gun at Maggie.

"No," Joe shouted.

From the woods behind the trailer, a shot rang out and Liam charged from his hiding place in the trees. Virgil dropped the pack and ran for his car as Liam and Jingles burst from the foliage, sprinting toward him. Virgil did not return fire, instead leaping into his vehicle and peeling out of the drive in a shower of gravel.

Maggie gulped back the fear and pounded up the steps to the trailer. "Tammy!" she screamed. The door slammed wide and she groped for a light.

Frantically she searched the bathroom and closet and even under the bed. She sank to her knees and began to sob. Her sister was not there.

* * *

Liam helped Maggie to a chair in the trailer and tried his best to comfort her. His head was whirling. He'd managed a quick call to Helen on the way over. She'd confirmed that Tammy was gone and she had no idea how. The thought that Virgil might have waltzed into the Lodge unnoticed sickened him. He might have hurt Tammy, Helen, any of the guests, to get what he wanted.

"We have to call the police," he said.

Joe shook his head. "Virgil will kill her. He said so."

Liam worked to keep his voice calm. "Joe, he didn't get what he wanted. He may take that action anyway."

Joe shook his head. "No. He hasn't gotten the jewelry." He flashed an angry look at Maggie. "Why did you try to trick him with an empty box? What were you thinking?"

"You're not going to badger her now," Liam growled. "The cops know how to handle things like this."

"I..." Joe started. His phone rang and his mouth slackened. "It's Virgil."

"Put it on speakerphone," Liam said, jaw tight.

"Nice trick," Virgil said. The words were

composed but Liam heard the quick panting that indicated he was on the verge of losing control. "I guess we're even. You didn't bring the jewelry and I didn't bring Tammy. We're going to try this again, one more time. If I don't get what I want, I will kill Tammy and then I will hunt Maggie down and murder her, too. I'll tell you the time and place next time I call."

"How do we know you even have Tammy?" Liam said. Proof of life. That's what they needed.

"Maggie…" One word, two anguished syllables cut off quickly, but not so fast that Liam couldn't hear the strain in her voice.

"Understand now?" Virgil said. "She's alive. They're both alive, until you double-cross me." The phone disconnected.

Liam sank to his knee in front of her. "Maggie, this is a police thing now. They know what to do."

"No," Joe said, the word sounding torn from him. "He'll kill Tammy next time. I know it. Give him what he wants. Her life isn't worth some diamond jewelry. If you think you can trick him with that empty box…"

"That's enough for now." Liam helped her to her feet. "I'll take her home. She'll decide what she wants to do without pressure from either one of us."

"But…"

"Go home, Joe. If Virgil calls, text me right away." He gave him the cell number for the new phone Chad had found for him since his was beyond repair thanks to the salt water.

"What am I supposed to do in the meantime?"

"Wait to hear from us."

"But…"

Liam ignored him this time, leading Maggie out to the truck and easing her into the passenger seat.

She was wide-eyed and staring the whole way back to the ranch. When he settled her into a chair in the saddlery, she jerked a look at him.

"What…what should I do? Should I tell Joe we don't have the jewelry?"

He shook his head. "I think not."

"Why? He loves her."

"Because the less people who know, the better, and…"

"And you don't like him?"

"Not particularly."

She laughed bitterly. "Because he's in love with your ex?"

Liam blew out a breath. "Maggie, I would hope by now you know that my motive in helping out here isn't about my past with your sister."

She dropped her head and the tears started again. "I'm sorry. I'm…"

"Upset. Understandable." He swirled her hair away from her cheek and caught the trail of tears with his thumb. "If I could take this pain on my shoulders for you, I'd do it in a hot minute."

She still didn't look at him. "My sister must be so scared. I don't know what to do."

He tried again to reason with her about the police, but she only seemed to retreat further into her shell.

"All right," he said after a deep breath. "If you're not going to let the police in, then you have to let me help." He smiled. "We'll go all Green Beret on him."

She gave him a watery sliver of a smile. "Not candy diplomacy?"

"No, ma'am," he said. "What I have in store for him is anything but sweet."

"Liam," she whispered, "are you sure this will work?"

"Certain as the sunrise," he said, praying deep down that his words were true.

TWENTY-ONE

Just before noon, he found Maggie haggard and jittery, pacing circles on the floor. She could not be enticed to eat, but he managed to get her to drink a couple sips of coffee. He drank some himself. He should eat something, but nothing awakened his appetite. He felt every sore muscle and hitched sinew, courtesy of the mighty Pacific.

His pulse jumped when the new phone buzzed with a call.

"He wants to meet tonight at the festival," Joe said. "At the Train of Lights, eight o'clock, with the jewelry."

Liam was not surprised. Plenty public so Virgil could blend in with the crowd. "Okay. How do we find him?"

"We don't. He'll find us." He heard Joe's quick breathing. "So what is the plan?"

"The plan is we do what he says." *To a point.*

Joe heaved out a breath. "And in the meantime we're just supposed to pretend like nothing's happened?"

"That's correct," Liam said. He clicked off.

Maggie looked shaky but strong enough. "So we spend the day on business as usual?"

"Best idea, in case Virgil's got eyes on us somehow. The whole town will be at the festival for the food and caroling tonight. Then trolleys are scheduled to transport groups from the Lodge to the station to get on the train." He was speaking as much for himself as for her, planning in his mind how to best use Mitch and Chad. "I'm going now to do some reconnaissance and scope things out with my brothers. You can stay here and rest."

"I don't need rest. I'm going to the Lodge, too, in case…oh, I don't know. I just want to be there."

He scrambled ahead of her outside and opened the passenger door of his truck. "I'll take you. Get in."

"Thank you, but I'll go myself."

"No. Why would you think that's a good idea?"

She sighed. "It's just easier to…"

To not be around me? He thought about his last heartfelt conversation with her. *Don't care for me….*

"Maggie," he said, closing his eyes for a second and striving for control. "Your knee is hurt and you've been through a trauma. Virgil is a loose cannon. The common sense thing is to let me give you a ride. Get in the truck." He paused. "Please."

He thought she would decline but, after a moment, she climbed in.

His palms were clammy on the steering wheel. What should he say? He wanted to keep the topic away from the panic she had to be experiencing about Tammy. He settled on, "How are you feeling? I mean, physically? Knee okay?"

"Banged up, but I'll live." She didn't look at him. "How about you?"

He shrugged, intending to feed her some macho "only a scratch" kind of comment. Instead he blew out a breath. "Actually, I imagine this is what a bowling pin feels like after a strike."

She stared for a moment, then smiled. "Thanks for the honesty."

It felt good to have made her smile again, with a frank assessment, no less.

She twisted to check on Jingles. "I'm glad you're okay, too, Jingles. Haven't eaten your candy cane yet?"

"Seems like he's saving it for a rainy day."

The rest of their chatter quieted until he

pulled up at the Lodge. Before she could hop out, he stopped her.

"Listen, I, uh… I mean, I know this has been sort of a nightmare and all, but I—I'm glad I… I mean, I'm happy I can be here to help you." As the words left his mouth he knew he'd cemented his title as "grand idiot." She'd offered her heart and he'd provided her a helpmate. What a dope.

She gave him a smile, shy and composed. "Me, too. Friends are hard to come by. Maybe we can stay in touch…"

"In touch? Are you leaving?"

"Before… I mean, last night, before he took her, I'd been making some plans." She swallowed. "I am going to talk to Tammy about where we should go from here."

"No need to go, is there?"

"I've already overstayed my welcome at the ranch."

"You're not…"

She shook her head. "If somehow we manage to get out of this alive…" She stopped and started again. "If Tammy is okay and not sent to jail, I'll return to Arizona. I'll stay as close as I can for as long as I can, but it won't be here in Driftwood. That's the only scenario I'm permitting myself to consider right now."

"It's gonna be okay," he said. "We'll get her

back and Virgil is the one who's going to jail. So you'll be able to live in Tammy's trailer."

"She's only paid up until the end of December."

"Extend it, maybe?"

"Liam," she said, rounding on him, "I don't want to stay here. There are just too many...uncomfortable memories."

And many of them revolved around him. He realized his mouth was open, so he shut it. He'd not offered her a single slim reason to stay, so why should she? He tried for composure before he answered. "Okay, I get it. Let me know if I can help, at all, with anything."

She'd gotten out of the truck before he could get the door for her and limped away toward the Lodge. Each step she took opened up miles between them. He felt powerless to stop her. What could he say? What had he to offer? The best he could do was use his skills and leverage those of his clan to get Tammy back safe and sound. As far as Maggie went, he could not shake the notion that he'd blown the best chance he'd ever had at happiness.

Jingles crammed his wedge of a head between the seats and licked Liam's ear, whining.

"I know, buddy," Liam said, heart in his boots. "I know."

The Chuckwagon van was parked at the side

entrance where Nan hefted boxes of pies. Maggie hurried over to assist, and he followed her and grabbed an armful. Stacks of apple, pumpkin and pecan pies scented the air. They were still warm, which made his mouth water. Maggie's cheeks were flushed, not from the effort of loading the van but because of his presence, he suspected, and the terrible strain she was under.

"I got this, Liam. You don't have to stay with me."

"You need some help."

"I don't." She pulled more boxes from the cargo area. "And I know you have other things to do."

"Mitch and Chad will be here in an hour. We'll work out the fine points. I'll fill you in when I know more, okay? In the meantime, I can help."

She slammed the back doors. "I just need to get these pies into the courtyard."

"I'll follow you."

"Like I said, you don't need to babysit me." Her lip quivered.

He raised his palms and offered her what he hoped was a comforting smile. "Helen always tells me to make myself useful. I do what I'm told."

She huffed out a breath and he backed off, finding an unobtrusive spot from which to watch her and memorize the tram schedule. He noted the guests had already started to filter out to enjoy the singing and warm cider.

A few vendors, including Yoriko, offered some last-minute gift items. As Maggie carried stacks of plates from the kitchen to the food tables, he passed knitted blankets, bead necklaces, ornaments and candles of every Christmas hue. On his last trip, he saw Maggie's attention caught by a slim beaded bracelet with a small gold heart. After a second glance, she walked by, to all appearances composed.

He wasn't sure how she was even still functioning. If anything happened to Helen, he would be losing his mind. But Maggie was like that, calm, strong, that steady presence in the middle of the storm, like the lighthouse beacon that shone no matter how vicious the hurricane. He looked again at the bracelet she'd noticed, feeling an intense desire to see it on her delicate wrist, wondering if it would make her smile.

A parting gift, a friendship token, he told himself as he peeled off a few bills and bought the bracelet while Maggie wasn't looking.

Time passed in slow motion. Maggie waited while Helen finished explaining the trolley schedule to a guest. Mitch and Chad might have arrived but she saw no sign of them. Could a former US marshal, an ex–Green Beret and a shy cowboy actually rescue her sister? Another wave of terror passed through her.

"It's a three-ring circus here," Helen said, walking around the desk to greet Maggie. "Every year we think we've considered everything, but there are always a million details to finish up." Helen gazed through the lobby doors into the courtyard where Maggie had delivered her pies. Strings of lights latticed the space that was crowded with a small stage where a costumed caroling group was warming up. The vendors had decorated their spots with tinsel, pine boughs and ribbons.

Maggie sighed. It should be a festive celebration but joy felt so very far away.

"The first trolley leaves at six," Helen called to a guest. "Enjoy the festivities." Helen beamed another smile, then moved away from the bustle. She touched a hand to Maggie's arm, the skin freezing cold. Helen might look as though she was calm and collected, but she could not completely hide her distress, perhaps her fear over what would unfold over the next few hours. "Tell me exactly what happened at the beach and Tammy's trailer."

Maggie did, watching terror and disappointment wash over Helen. "So Virgil thinks you found the jewelry, which is why he took Tammy.

I feel terrible. I woke up in the middle of the night to get a glass of water and I didn't bother to turn on the lights. I might have noticed that she was gone. In the morning, I just assumed she was out with Joe."

"You couldn't have known."

A great ripple of grief distorted Helen's features. "That's what everyone told me when my friend Fiona was murdered. It happened almost three years ago, but it feels like yesterday."

They gripped hands for a moment. "I'm sorry," Helen breathed. "Liam assures me that everything is going to be fine, but I know you're terrified."

She was too unsettled to reply.

Helen forced out a shaky breath. "Liam is the only person I'd want in my corner. He's a man you can count on and I know he cares about you deeply."

Cares? Maybe, but not in the way she desperately wanted. Maggie nodded and turned to leave. "I'll go make myself useful serving pie."

Helen stopped her. "Maggie, thank you for taking care of my brother the other night." Her lip trembled just for an instant before she regained her composure. "He's so afraid to give up control, and going deaf is his worst nightmare."

Maggie gripped Helen's fingers. "I hope

someday he can find a soul mate to share his burdens with."

Helen cocked her head. "I thought maybe he had, with you."

Maggie tried to swallow the lump in her throat. "We're...friends. That's all he wants."

"No, it's not," Helen said.

Maggie did leave then, trudging by the stairs, her heart twinging at the thought of what her sister might be enduring. Or maybe Virgil had already killed Tammy. She went cold inside. The thought that she could not help her sister, rescue her, even talk to her, stabbed like a knife. Powerless. It made her think how Liam must feel. Tammy was drowning in her own ocean and Maggie could not find a way to reach her.

The crowds kept coming, a sea of faces talking, laughing, their joy mingling with the Christmas carols and the cries of the children.

Hang on, Tammy. Just stay alive.

TWENTY-TWO

The trolley started off at sundown, ferrying groups to the station where they would board the Train of Lights. Mitch was already scouring the woods around the station. Chad would linger in the crowd, with eyes peeled for Virgil, and Liam would be a few steps away from Maggie, as close as he could get. He'd exchanged his cowboy hat for a baseball cap and his barn jacket for a long-sleeved plaid shirt. He wasn't going to carry a concealed weapon into a crowded place—too much potential for accidental injury to bystanders—but his rifle was with the truck and he knew his brothers had their weapons close by, as well. They would be ultracautious before using them.

Maggie had worked diligently all day, serving pie and cleaning up. He knew she took comfort in the activity. The strain showed on her face, her rigid posture, the way she clenched her hands and shoved them into the pockets of the red sweater she wore. A couple of hours and it would all be over.

Helen caught him in a quiet corner as he watched Maggie.

"You're going to be careful, right?"

He grinned. "'Course. Aren't I always?"

"No, would you like me to recite a list of the times you've been reckless? There was the moment when you decided you could evict the raccoon family from the attic with a broom all by your lonesome."

He poked her shoulder. "All right. Point taken. No need to run down all my bone-head moves."

She went quiet. "Liam, I mean it. It was bad enough worrying about you every single day when you were deployed. I can't do this life thing without my big brother."

He smothered her in a mighty hug. "You won't have to. I promise," he said into her hair.

"But, Liam…" He saw her gaze drift to Maggie.

"Gotta go," he said to forestall a comment he saw brewing in her eyes.

After a sigh, she kissed his cheek, raised her chin and sailed away into the crowd, to all appearances unruffled and serene while he went back to his silent watch. He allowed himself a moment to offer God a sincere thanks that he'd wound up with an exceptional sister like Helen.

I love you, sis.

A memory flashed through him of the three of them—his father, Helen and him—standing in front of his mother's empty chair the day after her funeral. His father had looked as though he'd wanted to say something, to offer some comfort to his grieving children. Liam remembered hearing him gulp and then bring Liam's hand to Helen's to join them together. Perhaps he'd been telling them, without words, that he could not be the one to kept the family intact; his grief was too much, his guilt overwhelming. Yes, his father had failed them, but he'd also reminded them in that one gesture that they had each other, a gift from God, solace and strength. Tears blurred Liam's eyes and he blinked them away as a weight he hadn't noticed before lifted.

Solace and strength. Better together.

The hours ticked on until Maggie headed to her place in line for the trolley. He stopped her and pretended to give her a hug and a Christmas greeting as he handed her a hefty pouch. "Decoy," he said. "Some grade-A gravel from out back of the Lodge, but I'm hopeful Virgil will think it's jewelry."

She flicked him a brief smile and stuffed the pouch into her pocket. "What if he doesn't bring her to the meet, like last time?"

"He's keeping her someplace close, has to be,

and I got his license plate when he grabbed the backpack. Rental car, but they have GPS trackers. I enlisted some help to check that out, in addition to Mitch and Chad."

"Help?"

He smiled. "Force multiplier, remember? I know people. He won't get away this time."

Her breath hitched. "Thank you. Your family means everything to you. It's kind of you to enlist them."

You mean everything to me. The thought skimmed through his mind easily like a horse racing through the green grass of the ranch. Flickers of memory shot through him.

The waves.

The fear.

Her palms on his cheeks.

The steady comfort in her eyes that was not pity.

The knowledge that his father had taught him something important, standing there in front of his mother's chair, spoken with his touch, just like Maggie had when he'd gone deaf after the explosion.

You'll learn to hear in other ways, with people to help you.

Feelings simmered in him that he'd never experienced before, begging to be let out, shared.

He clamped down on his rampaging thoughts. He had a job to do and her future hung in the balance.

"I'll be right there with you the whole time," he said into her ear, his lips touching the silken skin of her temple. And then she was boarding the trolley. He waited until a couple dozen people got on before he followed.

It was time for Virgil to learn a long overdue lesson.

Maggie disembarked with the throng at the train station. The railings were twined with Christmas lights and the old steam train itself was shimmering with tinsel and more lights. All around her people were strolling around taking pictures, queuing up behind the gate to be let on the train, exchanging hugs and handshakes. Music trilled and squealing children tugged at their parents' hands. Maggie scanned every person that came close, straining toward each young woman she saw, praying to catch a glimpse of her sister. She noted Liam standing in the shadows and she felt a bit braver.

Joe had given her his phone to use after being ordered to stay away by Liam. She did not think Joe was going to follow directions, since he'd looked as overwrought as she'd felt when they'd last talked.

The phone buzzed and she answered it.

"Mags…"

Maggie stopped breathing. "Tammy? Where are you?"

"In the back of the train," she whimpered. "He snuck on before anyone else. Please—"

She was running as the phone disconnected, past the throngs of Christmas celebrants, through the great plume of steam that erupted from the engine, hopping over the short railing. Gravel crunched under her shoes as she sprinted parallel to the tracks. Gasping for breath, she searched, nerves flooded with adrenaline.

The rear of the train was dark, until she caught a gleam from the last car, the flash of a light-colored shirt. Maggie scrambled up the nearest stairs and into the rear car. She pushed through the empty aisle and heaved open the door, emerging onto a small ledge caged by iron railings that overlooked the tracks. Her sister was wedged in the darkest corner.

"Tammy," she cried. Tears started in her eyes as she reached for her sister. "It's okay, honey. It's okay." She frantically felt for the ropes that tied Tammy to the railing.

"Sister comes to the rescue," came a voice from below.

Virgil stepped from the shadows, his gun trained on Tammy. He stood on the train track, a smile on his face. There was nothing Maggie could do except try to shield her sister from the line of fire.

"Throw me the jewelry," he said. "Quickly."

Maggie thought she saw a flicker of movement from the gloom. Liam? She pulled the pouch of gravel from her pocket. "Here, take it and leave her alone. You got what you wanted." She tossed the pouch to Virgil, intending to make him lunge for it, but he was too quick, snatching it from the air.

"This isn't another one of your tricks?"

She swallowed. "It's there. You'd better get away quick before someone sees you."

"I'd love to let it go, but there are too many witnesses now," he said, hefting the pouch in his palm.

Her blood froze. He was going to kill them anyway. She tried to edge farther in front of Tammy, but her sister pushed back, realizing what was about to happen, squirming and thrashing.

"Shouldn't you check it?" Maggie called in desperation, trying a different tact. "Maybe I'm trying to pull a fast one again. If you kill us first, you'll never know where the jewelry is hidden."

"Oh, I'm going to check it, all right." He pulled at the strings with his teeth.

The movement again from the shadows.

Virgil started to look over.

"How did you convince Bill to take out the life insurance policy?" Maggie blurted.

"He's not thinking too clearly since the old lady died," Virgil said after he opened the sack. He bent his head to peek inside.

In that one moment while his attention wavered a fraction, Liam leaped out from his hiding place and delivered a fist to Virgil's chin. It spun him back a step but didn't knock him down.

The sack went flying, gravel spewing in all directions. Virgil let out a cry of rage.

"What's wrong, Virg?" Liam said. "Didn't get your way?"

"I figured Maggie wouldn't come without her cowboy," Virgil said. "But I have backup, too." A shot from a distance pinged off the iron railing with a scatter of golden sparks.

Liam rolled, shouting, "Get down, Maggie."

As another shot cracked through the night, she tried to shelter her sister with her body, crouching as low as they could. There was more shouting and the beams of flashlights bounced over the ground. When Maggie looked up, she could see only dark silhouettes locked in a wrestling match below.

"Liam?" Her question was swallowed up by the hiss of steam.

* * *

Liam registered the fact that the secondary shooter was a mighty poor marksman. Virgil's backup hadn't done the job. Liam got off one quick punch that sent Virgil stumbling back. Then they went at it in earnest. He was surprised at Virgil's strength, but he persisted, throwing a forearm across Virgil's throat. Gasping and choking, Virgil finally surrendered and Liam rolled him over onto his stomach, a knee between his shoulder blades. Chad came running past the confused crowd and handed him a rope with which he tied Virgil's wrists behind his back and secured him to a lamppost for good measure.

"Text Mitch to look for the second shooter," Liam panted.

Chad complied.

Liam scrambled up the train steps to the women, cutting through Tammy's bonds with his pocketknife. He handed Tammy down the steps to Chad and took Maggie's arm to lead her. She did not take her eyes off her sister.

Chad stayed with Tammy and Maggie and kept watch over Virgil while Liam checked the area thoroughly, calling Danny Patron, as well. There was no sign of the second shooter, only the trail of headlights as a car sped away from the station.

Liam ground his teeth, praying his older brother had been able to intercept Virgil's cohort. He jogged back to the train station to find Danny Patron pulling up, red lights flashing.

After a quick briefing, Danny dispatched an officer to check the train and surrounding area thoroughly before he finally allowed the celebrants to board. Liam returned to the women and Chad, settling in for a tongue-lashing from the police chief. Tammy was no longer crying, but Maggie still crooned words of comfort to her.

"And furthermore," Danny said, chin set in aggravation, "if you're gonna go all cowboy in the future, at least give me the courtesy of joining in the fun."

"Yes, Chief," Liam said. "I will."

As the train lurched along the track, Mitch arrived on horseback. He leaned on his saddle horn. "Nothing."

Liam let out a groan. "That's not the news I wanted to hear."

Danny looked closely at the bound Virgil. "Is that a glove in his mouth?"

"Yes, sir," Chad said. "He was using some awful inappropriate language in front of the ladies."

Danny laughed. "Very considerate of you."

"Don't mention it," Chad said.

Liam texted Helen whom he knew would be in agony. She called him immediately.

"Bring them straight here to the Lodge, Liam. Maggie will want to stay the night with her sister. I'll make room. Joe just showed up and he's frantic to see her, too." She hung up but not before he heard the wobble in her voice. It pained him that she'd been scared, that Virgil had ever caused her a single moment of distress. The sisters didn't argue as he got them on the next empty trolley en route to the Lodge.

"Virgil's really going to jail?" Tammy said, shuddering. "Will I go, too? Will Bill believe what his nephew has done?"

Liam squeezed her shoulder. "One thing at a time, but I'm confident Danny can persuade the judge to use some leniency if Bill doesn't come around." Since the trolley was vacant, he eased a seat away, allowing the women to comfort each other in those soft, gentle murmurings that were too low for him to catch. He didn't have to hear to understand, he realized with a start.

Maggie was right about him learning to hear in other ways. It was just another validation.

He swallowed a lump in his throat and thanked God for what he'd learned and what he had almost lost.

TWENTY-THREE

Maggie felt as though she was in a daze, sleep-walking through the empty lobby of the Lodge. Helen greeted them all with hugs and tears, settling them near the fire close to the massive decorated tree, and produced a tray of hot tea and mugs. Mitch and Chad had returned to the ranch. Virgil, the gun, her sister bound…it all seemed surreal, a terrifying nightmare. But here was Tammy alive and well. She could not have asked for a better result, if she could just get her brain to believe it.

She stared, blinking dumbly, at the sparkling silver ornaments that hung on each bough, reminding her of the jewelry Virgil had almost killed them to retrieve. She did not know what would happen to her sister legally, but she couldn't be too worried about that. Tammy was unhurt, as far as she could tell, her crying subsiding into spurts with sniffling in between.

"Tammy!" Joe ran into the room and Tammy threw herself into his arms, crying onto his shoulder.

"I'm okay," she said around her sobs. "He didn't hurt me."

Joe squeezed her close and Maggie and Liam moved away to give the couple some privacy.

"I'm going to go see if the cook can rustle up some soup," Helen said.

"I can help," Maggie said, earning a laugh from Helen.

"Oh, no, you most certainly cannot. You're going to sit and rest and recover. Period. I'm going to let Jingles loose. He's been whining since you leashed him in the dining room."

Helen strode off and Liam grinned. "Like I said, it's best to follow orders where Helen is concerned."

In a moment Jingles bounded into the room with an exuberant yip, sliding to a stop to receive a friendly scratch from Liam. "Hey, buddy. I told you I'd come back."

"Have you two become friends now that you've exchanged candy canes?" Maggie said.

He laughed. "Aw, he's growing on me."

She watched the dog wriggle around his master, completely devoted. Maggie felt her heart swell with gratitude.

"How can I thank you?" She realized Liam's

attention was still on the dog. She put a hand on his shoulder. "Liam, you saved my sister's life, not to mention mine."

Liam shrugged a shoulder. "Too bad the jewelry didn't turn up. I'm hopeful Tammy will get her memory back someday."

She started again to try to express her gratitude without being too personal. *Keep it light, like he wants.* Her attention was snagged away when Jingles trotted over and sprawled underneath the Christmas tree.

The branches shuddered as his tail raked the needles, sending the big glass ornaments on the bottom branches bobbing. The one that hung just above Jingles's head looked lower than it should, as if some strange weight was pulling it down. Maggie went over and removed it, holding it up to the light. Her breath caught in her throat.

"Tammy?" she said.

"Uh-huh?" Tammy answered, without taking her eyes off Joe.

"That night, when you came to the Lodge and Helen took you in, did you stay in the lobby for any length of time?"

"Yes. Helen told me to stay by the fire and warm up while she changed the bed in her room for me." She looked over. "Why?"

"Because I think I know where you hid the jewelry."

Maggie held the ornament up higher and the soft overhead light shone through the glass interior. Nestled inside was a tangle of diamond jewelry.

Tammy squealed in delight. "So that's what I did. I unhooked the top and fed the necklace and bracelets inside. I can't believe I didn't remember doing that." Her face broke into a massive smile. "Now we can give it back to Bill."

"It's—" Maggie broke off to stare at Joe, who had emitted a shocked cry. His pallor was stark white, his mouth slack with shock. Why shock? Surprise, certainly, but his expression was inexplicably troubled.

"What's wrong, Joe?" she asked.

"No," he said, shaking his head as if he hadn't heard. "It's not going back to Bill. It's for us, Tammy. You and me. That was the deal."

Tammy started at him. "What deal? What are you talking about?"

A snatch of conversation reverberated in Maggie's mind, something Virgil had said at the parade.

My sister would never be with someone like you, a greedy liar.

Are you so sure of that? Maybe your sister isn't as smart as you think.

Joe moved closer, hand out. "Give that to me, Maggie."

Tammy's mouth fell open. "Joe, what are you doing?"

Liam blew out a breath. "You were the one who was supposed to stage the theft. You and Virgil cooked up the plan together."

"It was his plan, but I went along with it. Even quit my job so we wouldn't be linked. He'd skim the insurance money and I'd get the necklace, fence it and keep the payoff." Joe turned desperate eyes on Tammy. "For our future, baby. You were never supposed to be involved, but then you took it. Virgil went after you. When I learned he'd driven you off the road, I was furious, but he said we could clean the whole thing up if I helped him find the jewelry."

"Was it you at the lighthouse?" Liam demanded.

"No," Joe said. "All I did was follow you and try to get the backpack at the beach."

"You almost drowned Liam and Maggie." Tammy's face was aghast.

"The Corvette," Liam continued. "That was your work, too, wasn't it? Virgil had an alibi."

Joe's mouth tightened but he continued to gaze at Tammy, his expression pleading. "I didn't want to kill anyone. If I hadn't done what he'd said, he'd have come after Tammy himself.

Don't you see?" He turned pleading eyes on Tammy. "I had to ensure our future."

"A real man," Liam said with a snort. "And you were the second shooter at the train station, weren't you?"

"The shot wasn't anywhere close. I wouldn't risk hurting Tammy."

"Doesn't matter, Joe," Liam said. "You're going to jail now with Virgil."

Joe hesitated and pulled a gun from his pocket. "No, I'm not."

Maggie felt her disbelief give way to fear as Joe turned to Tammy. "I love you. We can get out of here, go someplace together. The jewelry is worth a fortune. No one else has to get hurt. I did all this for you. For us. Now you can understand, right? Come with me."

"Oh," Tammy said, eyes brimming, voice throbbing with betrayal. "Too late for that. I'm not going anywhere with you."

He grimaced. "I've gone too far now, Tammy. I can't go back. Don't you see? I have to get away. Please come with me. We can start over somewhere new after we sell the jewelry."

Maggie tried to snatch at her sister as Tammy stepped closer to him. "I wouldn't go anywhere with you. I was completely blind not to see what you were doing before."

Joe sucked in a breath and aimed the gun at

Maggie. "Give it to me. I don't want to hurt you, or anyone, but I have no more options."

Maggie held the ornament up. "All this deceit and threats and ultimatums for something that never belonged to either of you."

Joe's lips tightened into a grimace. "Save it. Give me the ornament."

"Okay. Here you go." Maggie lobbed it at Joe, higher than he was expecting. It sailed over his head and Helen snagged it, a reflexive catch, as she reappeared in the lobby.

With Joe off balance from his lunge, Tammy flung out a foot and swept his legs out from under him. He fell back with a grunt. Liam was on him in a moment, fingers locked on Joe's wrists. Jingles barked and bit down on Joe's pant leg, yanking and tugging for all he was worth. They rolled into the tree and it wobbled, nearly overturning. Neither Jingles nor Liam loosened their holds and, in a moment, it was all over. Liam wrestled the gun free and sent it skidding across the floor. Maggie raced over to make sure the gun stayed out of reach. Liam rolled Joe onto his stomach and knelt on him, breathing hard.

Helen stared from the prostrate Joe to her brother to the glass ornament in her palm that glittered and sparkled with its hidden treasure. Her look of surprise shifted to pure wonder.

"Well, now," Liam said with a grin. "I'd say that was a fine group effort, wouldn't you?"

"Yes," Helen said. "I'm sure glad you taught me how to catch, Liam."

Liam chuckled as he got to his feet. "You can be on my team any day."

Maggie was torn between a laugh and a sob as she embraced her sister.

Danny Patron took Joe into custody and loaded him into the squad car.

"And they say nothing happens in Driftwood," he said with a chuckle. "I spoke to the DA, just to be sure, but he concurs that there should be no reason Tammy should face any jail time."

Liam clasped his hand in a grateful shake and watched him drive away.

He wandered into the empty courtyard where the festival had been in full swing only a short while earlier. What a difference a couple of hours could make. He stood behind Maggie as she gazed out across the courtyard bedazzled with Christmas lights. It was silent now, the lull before the bustle of the guests returning from their train trip, unaware of what had transpired at the station and Lodge. He was in no hurry for the moment to end as he gazed at Maggie. She was quite simply beautiful, profile gilded by the lights, expression pensive. He shoved his hands into his pockets to keep from reaching for her, finding the beaded bracelet he'd forgotten he'd purchased.

He sidled up next to her and she gave him a wan smile.

"Processing it all?"

She nodded. "Trying to figure out what's next. Tammy's going to stay in her trailer for a while until she gets her bearings again. She's heartbroken, for sure. I need to be with her until the shock wears off."

"Absolutely." He added quickly, "For support and all."

"She really loved him."

"Yes. That hurt's not going to heal quickly."

Maggie frowned. "Helen offered me a job at the Lodge as a chef. I'm not sure what to do."

"I am." The words erupted before his brain thought them through. This time he did not need to hide behind a quip or witticism. For the first time in a long while he was sure—dead certain—and completely comfortable with the decision he was about to reveal to her. He took her wrist and slid on the bracelet. "A Christmas present."

"Oh," she said. "How pretty. I didn't…get you anything."

He quirked a grin. "Pancakes. Those are way better than presents."

She smiled, eyeing the bracelet again. "Well, I love it, thank you."

"I should be thanking you." He cleared his throat.

Her eyes reflected the glow of the light strings. "Why? It seems like—"

"I'm scared," he said flatly, cutting her off.

She gaped at the admission, startled into silence.

"I'm scared, Maggie." He gulped in some air, partly in disbelief that he'd gone ahead and spoken it. It was time. It was right. "Terrified, actually, of losing my hearing."

She moved a bit toward him, but he stopped her again. "I haven't said those words since I was seven years old."

"It's okay. You don't have to…"

"But I'm saying them with you because—" he sucked in a breath and steeled his spine "—I trust you. I mean, I trust you like no one else. I've never allowed myself to cultivate that kind of trust before."

Her smile was sweeter than a summer's day. "I'm so glad but… I mean, I know Tammy's single again now…"

"And we'll always be friends. But that's it. It's different with you." He cleared his throat.

"You make me believe that I will survive going deaf one day."

Tears glimmered on her lashes. One spilled down her cheek and he caught it with his thumb.

"And you were right," he went on in a rush. "God meant us to do life together and… I know that you and I are supposed to…" He went all hot and thick inside, and the words stuck in his throat until she looked at him with that green-gold gaze that spoke of autumns and acceptance and gentle strength and rock-solid faith. What a woman she was and oh, how he wanted her to be his forever.

He gave up on the spoken words. Instead he stilled his shaking hands and made the sign that Charlie had showed him. With awkward effort, he put up his thumb, forefinger and pinky, ring and middle finger down. One more breath, palm out, moving his hand slightly from side to side, he told her without a single word.

I love you.

He heard her breath hitch, saw the tears begin to spill down her cheeks in earnest.

"I love you, too, Liam," she whispered. "So much more than I can ever say."

"Merry Christmas, Maggie," he choked out as he took her in his arms.

"Merry Christmas, Liam," she whispered back.

Jingles scampered over and sat. Liam looked

in astonishment at the bunch of candy canes clenched in his mouth. "Where in the world did he find those?"

Maggie laughed. "He brought extras this time, one for each of us."

Overflowing with joy, Liam reached for her, holding her in his arms and relishing the freedom he felt as his heart expanded, doubled over and wrapped him in a glow lovelier than any lavish holiday display.

He found her lips with his and joined their lives together with a perfect Christmas kiss.

* * * * *

*If you enjoyed this story,
look for the first book in
the Roughwater Ranch Cowboys series
by Dana Mentink:*

Danger on the Ranch

Dear Reader,

I am writing this letter as I sit in a bustling hospital emergency room, waiting for some test results for a family member. Time seems to slow down here, the conversations ebbing and flowing around me in this busy place. It strikes me that we have so many ways to quantify a human life, don't we? We can measure the beats of the heart, the actions of enzymes, the microbes and platelets and pulses and respirations that keep a body alive. For all that, we cannot measure a person's capacity to love, the intangible desire of one person to care deeply for another. That, my friends, is the beautiful inheritance from the Lord. He gives us the ability to love, because He first loved us. What a treasure, what a gift.

Thank you so much for reading my story. I hope it entertained and inspired you. Most of all, I hope you feel deeply that you are loved by our Father. If you'd like to contact me, feel free to send a note via my website at danamentink. com. There is also a physical address there if you prefer corresponding by letter. As always,

God bless you, my friends, and thank you for joining me on this adventure!

Sincerely,

Dana Mentink

Get 4 FREE REWARDS!

We'll send you 2 FREE Books <u>plus</u> 2 FREE Mystery Gifts.

Harlequin® Heartwarming™ Larger-Print books feature traditional values of home, family, community and—most of all—love.

FREE
Value Over
$20